INCREDIBLE ACCLAIM FOR CASEY MARX'S

360 to PARADISE

"Casey Marx's *360 to Paradise* explodes out of the gate with a fury and intensity rarely matched. From page one to the end, it is heart-pounding, non-stop action. Move over Holden Caulfield and Jack Kerouac, your number is up. The new rebel in town is Cody Reese, destined for literary immortality. This book was so compelling and engaging, I couldn't put it down. It's a triumph on every level. A breath-taking debut by a fresh, new American voice."-**David Assael**, *award-winning novelist and writer of Saint Elsewhere, Miami Vice, Star-Trek: The Next Generation and Northern Exposure. His film, "Evan's Crime", is winning rave reviews on the film festival circuit. And his latest movie, The Jade Pendant, just finished shooting in Salt Lake City, Utah.*

"*FAST TIMES AT RIDGEMONT HIGH* meets *BREAKING BAD.* Casey Marx has INVENTED A NEW FORM—the SCRIPT-NOVEL. A fresh, balls-out look into the Dark Soul of PARADISE aka SANTA BARBARA, CA."-**James Kahn**, *author of Poltergeist and The Goonies.*

"Casey Marx's prose is kinetic, alive, and the pages roar along FASTER THAN A BULLET TRAIN. His protagonist is a latter-day HUNTER S. THOMPSON rolled into HOLDEN CAULFIELD, a 'SHAMAN TO THE NEXT DIMENSION.'"-**Robert Eisele**, *WGA award-winning screenwriter of The Great Debaters.*

ABOUT THE AUTHOR

Casey Marx is a filmmaker with over ten years experience shooting and editing primetime documentaries for MTV, Discovery, Showtime and NBC. He's made videos for several Grammy-award winning artists, from Tim McGraw, T-Bone Burnett, to reggae-ska legend Tippa Irie. Casey has directed videos for chart-topping acts including Dada Life, O.T. Genasis, Mickey Avalon, and the Pharcyde, which have millions of views. He graduated from the Tisch School of the Arts at New York University and lives in Los Angeles.

360 to PARADISE

Casey Marx

Cover Design by Geneva Robertson-Dworet and Sam Mayle.

www.caseymarx.com

360 to Paradise / Casey Marx. -- 1st ed.

ISBN 978-0-9967452-0-8

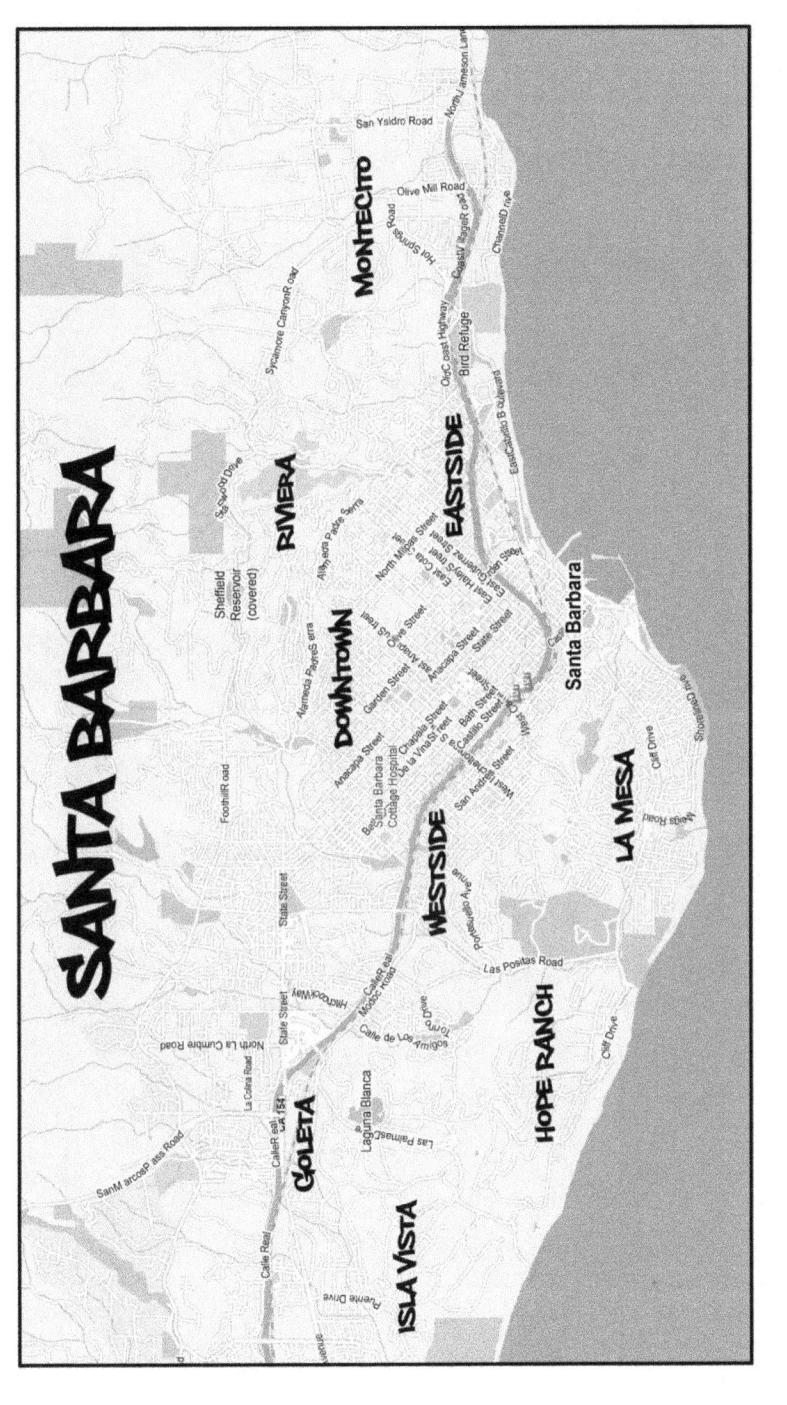

"Who gives a fuck about tomorrow?"

—surf & skate mantra

Chapter ONE

Where the Fuck am I?

8:19 am

I coughed, grabbing my head. I was hurting. Hung over. On the bedside table I saw a humongous bottle of cheap Russian Vodka. Just the sight of it made me kinda nauseous. I spotted a glass of orange-ish liquid.
Dying of thirst, I took a sip.
Ugh!

I spit it back into the cup and watched my saliva slowly drool down. I peeked around, trying to figure out where the hell I was.

Earth didn't feel like a safe bet.

I'm eighteen. Bleach-blond dreadlocks. And enough pigment in my skin so you know not to fuck with me.

I've been called a wetback. Cursed out for being black. Even been accused of being a Chinese Albanian.

Maybe I'm just a regular white guy with a killer surf tan?

And no, it's not just my nose ring that makes me a rebel. Take one look in my eyes.

You'll see I'm not afraid. To throw a middle finger. At any authority figure.

Be it a cop.

Or President mutherfuckin' Obama.

I'm ready to conquer the world. But not today. At least, not yet, not till I'm a little more sober.

Guessing from the cut-outs of Diplo, Adam Levine, and Skrillex, I figured I was in the bedroom of some chick still trapped in her teens. On the desk were a few gifts wrapped in colorful paper. Balloons. A gigantic birthday card. The remains of an erotic cake—genitalia mashed and devoured.

I pulled down the covers and was pleasantly surprised to discover a beautiful girl snoring gently. She wore an oversized Seahawks jersey and a thong. But I had no idea who the fuck she was or how I got to be next to her.

I glanced back at the bedside table and saw a gooey-looking used condom. I celebrated with some wicked air drums—a really bitching solo. Then I quietly lifted up her shirt and checked out her rack.

Ma'am, you're going to have to check those.

Before I could really examine her lovely breasts, my phone vibrated like a possessed demon.

Reality calls.

I threw on my clothes. Super baggy shorts with mad room for my balls to hang and lots of pockets to hide contraband.

I grabbed my skateboard and backpack, blew my sweet princess a kiss, and jammed the hell outta there.

CHAPTER TWO

No Capacity in Hell

8:22 am

Damn. Fucking bright outside. I flipped on my shades and let them soak in all that terrible sun. I strolled down the driveway towards the street as a muscular MEXICAN DUDE, covered in tattoos, struggled to pull a massive TV from the back of his pickup truck. Dude oozed danger, like he just busted out of prison.

He whistled. "Mind giving me a hand with this kickass birthday present, homey?"

Could this banger be talking to me?

Normally, I wouldn't stop on my way to nowhere, but today I felt I owed the universe one after scoring last night. We struggled to pull the heavy TV out of the pickup, each of us lugging an end of the giant box towards the house.

"You rage with the babes last night?"

"Yeah, hurting, too." I let out a monster belch. "Someone must've slipped me a roofie cause I can't remember nada!"

"God, I miss nights like that! So which chick you slam? Britney? She's such a slut."

"Hmmm..." I tried to think but it was like trying to cut stale bread. "Fuck, I really declared jihad on my brain last night."

"You must've really been rocking 'n rolling! What color hair she have?"

"Blond." I licked my lips. "And real blond cause I checked. Walked through fields of gold, you feel me?"

"Wow, you've managed to make pussy sound gay," the dude grinned. "So, you nail Mandy? With nice little boobs?"

"Definitely not! That I do remember. Wait... did you say this is a birthday present?"

We locked eyes. *Oh, fuck. I just boned this vato's hyna!*

The TV crashed to the ground, shattering the screen. The dude yelled in fury as he picked up a huge rock and hurled it towards me. It narrowly missed, smashing into a car window.

"Dude!" I screamed, "You insane?!"

But I would've been crazy to wait to find out.

Instead, I hopped on my skateboard and pumped as quickly as my legs would push. The Dude jumped in his F-350, gunned the engine, and screeched after me.

"Play epic skate mix," I commanded my Apple Watch as I popped in my headset. A grinding anthem dedicated to snorting coke:

Every girl sips my champagne

Squeezes my chain,

Screams my name,

While I fuck their brains on their daddy's Mustang.

Pounding drums. Was like driving a screw through your skull. I fed off it, skating faster and faster.

The dude, screaming so loud I could hear it even over the raunchy lyrics, careened toward me. I expertly weaved onto the sidewalk. My eyes bulged—ahead of me, two ancient grannies approached, pushing heavy carts of groceries. I roared toward them with the fury of a nuclear missile.

"MOVE!!!!!!"

The old ladies somehow managed to stumble out of harm's way. I ripped past them, realizing I had to get off the sidewalk fast. Red construction signs loomed ahead. I channeled Shaun White, carving hard down a slippery driveway, and caught big air off the lip.

I landed hard and way too fast, compensating with bent knees lower than a Judo master. A van loaded with kids pulled out of a driveway right in front of the F-350.

The Dude slammed to a stop, cursing.

I smiled, carving ahead onto a dangerously steep hill. Double-black-diamond. Pros only. I tucked low and leaned back for max speed. Do or die, baby. The Dude, thundering behind, shouted, "I'm gonna feed you your own cajones, motherfucker!"

Damn it, an intersection. I tightened up on the board, nearly losing my balance, as I hit a wicked bump. My skateboard vibrated worse than an over-powered dildo.

I WAS OUT OF CONTROL!

A station wagon started making a left. The Driver couldn't see me until TOO LATE—

CRACK!

I smashed into the windshield like a spear from Satan, shattering the glass to bits. My vision swirled to a ghostly black. I fell limply onto the concrete.

For a few, long, terrifying seconds I lay on the street. Lifeless.

Suddenly, miraculously, I jolted back to life.

"YOU OK?" the Driver asked, but I was too dazed to say shit. My eyes struggled to focus on the Mexican and his F-350 rocketing towards me, plowing through garbage cans, knocking them over like bowling pins. I hopped back on my board and zoomed down an alleyway.

Ahead, the alley turned into a dead end. I was headed straight for a brick wall.

Showtime, baby. No posers!

At the last second I leaned hard into an epic turn and ollied high onto a ledge. I grinded a long concrete rail, bending my knees low again to maximize my pop, and BOOM—

I launched over a death-defying gap. I flailed my arms wildly, barely sticking the landing.

The F-350 smashed into the brick wall. Smoke erupted from the hood.

"FUCK YEAH!" Suddenly, I was on the—

CITY COLLEGE CAMPUS.

I melted into the hundreds of students wandering around, wasting time between class. I cruised past a group of super hot chicks. A blistering red-head with a body built for a magazine cover tried to wave me down.

"Cody, baby! We gonna party tonight?"

I stared at Tinker Bell. Although everyone in town would build a pyramid for this beauty, I didn't have time to roll out the red carpet. I absorbed her insanely short skirt and murderous red stilettos. She belonged at Spearmint Rhino dancing on a pole rather than at ECON 101—

But hey, that's what Santa Barbara City College is all about.

I ripped across a bridge to the East Campus and the most insane view of the harbor and shimmering bay.

Welcome to Paradise, baby.

CHAPTER THREE

Junior Houdini

8:49 am

My teacher, a scorching hot babe on loan from Cartagena, rambled on in Spanish about different animals you might see at a zoo. "There are lions, tigers, and bears."

A chunky student with curly hair the same color as apricot jam squeezed another massive nacho full of sour cream into his mouth. "In this zoo, is there a pussy?" he asked.

"Un gato?"

Everyone in the class laughed except me.

I sat deep in the bleachers barely inhaling a word. A tattooed girl passed me her Spanish book. I popped it open. No, it wasn't the answers to last night's quiz. It was a crisp $50 bill. I nonchalantly pocketed the dinero and replaced it with a baby Ziploc full of white powder. I carefully slid the book across the linoleum without anyone batting an eye. The tattooed girl inspected the package and gave me a nod.

Another satisfied customer. Hey, chill.

I know exactly what you're thinking. Just cause I deal I must be a lowlife.

But you got it all wrong.

I have a strict code: never slang hard drugs—only party favors. Harmless chemicals that make people happy. Weed, coke, acid, shrooms, molly, moon rocks, sassafras, GHB, and sure, maybe a few Addy's and Xanny's if I can get my mitts on 'em. Need a gram of Special K to make the night fly?

And all you moral assholes who think I'm a scumbag are wrong. I help people unlock and explore the dark crevices of their minds. If someone decides to buy drugs from me, it's a consensual agreement amongst two adults. So yes, I'll be your mediator, baby. Your shaman to the next dimension.

I'm the Last of the Mohicans and the Last Man Standing!

Just me, and a backpack full of enough good times to blast you to the moon. Sure, I can put you in Ibiza or the Electronic Daisy Carnival. Just gimme two seconds. Here, swallow, snort, rip, shoot, and smoke your face off.

My phone alarm chirped. Time to take another pill cause under no circumstance can I afford to get locked up for cloudy piss. I pulled out a bottle of Herbal-Flush and popped a few giant capsules. I chugged them down with a massive gallon of water I'd been lugging around like a weight lifter. Fucking probation. Note to dumb-ass self: *don't get busted, again, EVER!*

The teacher turned her back, writing a lengthy assignment on the board. I whipped out a bottle of lighter fluid.

SHOWTIME!!

I slowly poured the fluid onto my hand. All the students around stared in disbelief. I pulled out my trusty Zippo and held it dangerously close to my soaked hand.

The tattooed chick grabbed me. "Fuck's into you?!"

The teacher turned, disturbed by the commotion. "Cody! PLEASE, STOP!!"

Perfect, I've got what I want. The whole class' attention.

I sparked the Zippo—

WHOOSH!

My hand erupted in wild flames. Students screamed, freaking the fuck out.

Calm, like a Jedi Master, I held my hand up, as though I had a 'burning question' for the hot teacher.

My classmates morphed into a cage of howling monkeys—the teacher cursed in Spanish, everyone jumped frantically away from my flaming hand, and the tattooed girl yelled as she grabbed the fire extinguisher.

"Wait!" I twisted my hand and suddenly, miraculously, 'Voilà!'

The fire vanished.

"Incredible, isn't it?" I showed off my hand for the students to inspect. "Not a single burn mark."

Everyone was mystified.

Satisfied, I casually flipped through my textbook like nothing happened.

Like my hand wasn't just on fucking fire.

The tattooed girl nudged me. "How'd you do that?"

My teacher glared.

"C'mon, you know you liked it too," I teased. All the students giggled and I was back in elementary school. Once the class clown, always the class clown.

And yeah, it was worth it then, too.

The teacher shook with fury. "Out! And I'd drop this course before tomorrow's deadline, unless you don't mind getting an F+."

"Duh? There is no F+." Again, the class laughed. I packed my textbook into my backpack as slow as humanly possible. I relished every second of the awkward silence. A few JOCKS high-fived me as I strutted toward the door. A neatly-folded paper airplane landed at my feet.

But I didn't need to guess who it was from. Only one friend likes to send messages the old school way. It read: "You're such an idiot. Meet me outside the bathroom!!"

CHAPTER FOUR

Addicted 2 Love

9:06 am

finished taking a leak in the toilet, flushing with a kick. On the wall written in pink lipstick: 'TAP YOUR FOOT TWICE FOR SEX-ED.' I ignored the generous offer, spotting some graffiti across the toilet paper dispenser:

PSYCHO 21

Douche-bag thinks he can hit up MY SCHOOL?

On the real, Psycho had a fresh style and his graffiti belonged in some esoteric-artsy blog or hanging at the Guggenheim. But, like my man Addict said before he died tagging a freeway overpass, "I'm out here to bomb, period. I didn't start writing to go to Paris. I didn't start writing to do canvasses. I started writing to bomb. Destroy all lines."

If Psycho 21 wanted to bring war, I was ready. I whipped out a thick, permanent marker. The fire in my belly flared, the adrenaline pumped like a metronome, and I crossed out Psycho's tag, covering it with my own:

CITO RATS!

I added a couple stars for flare before bouncing outside for a nice cigarette.

"Hey, stranger!"

Sajda cruised up behind me. She'd just turned eighteen, and although most thought her gorgeous butter pecan skin was her secret—it wasn't.

What really took my breath away was her mesmerizing smile. It was better than winning the lottery. I didn't care that her father raised her as a strict Muslim—which meant she always covered her hair. She wrote a provocative Muslim fashion blog under the name ESSRA and looked extra spicy today in mustard-yellow tights with a t-shirt that read:

I ♥ My Hijab

"You never texted back last night."

"Hmm." I licked my lips. "The message about sneaking in your house to tuck you in?"

She smiled. That gynormous smile I warned you about. "You got a vivid imagination."

"Isn't that why you like me? Cause I'm creative?" I scanned the perimeter for campus security. Satisfied, I reached into my satchel and pulled out a quarter of True O.G. Kush. "Here's that sack you wanted."

"I changed my mind. Logan said you're so creative you're back to selling coke. That true?"

I didn't answer.

"So, you're going on the record as only a weed dealer?"

"What'd you forget, the cameras and reporters? I would've brought my lawyer."

"We both know all you can afford is a Public Defender. So isn't it time to pull your head out of the clouds and get a real job?"

My Apple Watch rang loudly, interrupting her. I glanced at the number.

It was EMILIANO.

Goddamn, that muthafucker never gives up!

Sajda sighed, annoyed: "And you love that your stupid phone's always blowing up, don't you?"

I punched IGNORE, grabbed her fashion sketch book, and flipped through the pages.

She pointed to a few sketches of bright bikinis so colorful they burst off the page. "You're going to see some of these designs on tonight."

I threw her a look.

"Wait, you didn't forget my shoot, did you? You can't flake, Codes! No fucking way. It's enough my other two male models both simultaneously got the flu. You're my David Beckham. If ever I needed your help—this is it!"

"Better be careful. This could be the start of something huge." I struck a dramatic pose and held my face intently with my hands. "Don't you think I'm sexy??"

She grinned. Alright, got her back in my tractor beam. I reached for her hand but she pulled back.

"Remember," she whispered, "when my father was away—in San Diego—and you crashed at my house? But you didn't stay on the couch like you were supposed to."

"The floor was slanted. I fell off and rolled into your bedroom."

She hesitated—and suddenly, *I knew.*

This had happened before, but I didn't expect it from Sajda. You sleep with a girl and don't call her back and what do you know—she's in fucking love with you. Happens every time. Somehow I thought with Sajda it would be different. Just fun between friends.

"Don't get me wrong, you know I think you're the most amazing, beautiful girl, but—what do you want?"

"What?"

"I'm flattered, believe me."

"Cody—"

"You know me, I can't get serious—"

"What did you think I was about to say?"

I stopped. "That you... love me?"

"No, you idiot. I'm pregnant."

a few weeks ago:

A kaleidoscope of images battered and pummeled my brain. Of course I remembered that night. When Sajda and I got the party going, it didn't wanna go back in the bottle.

We were at an epic mansion rager in Hope Ranch. It belonged to a bigwig two billion dollar hedge fund manager—a Wall Street legend. *Luckily, the Legend was gone and the kids had taken over.* There were so many nooks and crannies and guesthouses to play in—Saj and I found our own private sauna to start our own ruckus. She kept pouring shots till we were well past ga-ga-land.

"We're celebrating my acceptance to Fashion Institute of Design in Manhattan! You heard back from any colleges?"

"Not yet." I hated myself for lying to the only person in the whole world who really had my back.

"Give it a day or two, those giant college acceptance envelopes will be overflowing your mailbox."

I didn't know what to tell her.

The truth? Would she respect that?

She poured another round of shots. "We're not Cito kids with diamond-studded iPads. All we have is each other. If you don't get accepted, I'm not going to New York."

We both slammed our drinks down.

"When you gonna get your shit together, Codes?"

"I'm stacking paper, baby."

"If you were REALLY STACKING, wouldn't you have a car?"

Saj always smashed me with a fistful of truth. And there was no running cause she always caught me in her net.

"You win, homey." I gave her a knuckle pound. It still didn't feel weird to treat her like a "bro." You know, pound her knuckles instead of giving her a hug like every other chick. I called her my homey. My *ese*.

Even my brother.

"But we weren't just stoned. Or crazy," she said. "Didn't we always plan to get the hell out of Santa Barbara? And go to New York together? Cause it's way less scarier if you go with someone you know—and trust."

I took a long moment. Digesting the sad thought of her packing up and leaving. We'd both dreamed of going. Now, she was. And I'd become—

God—

What the fuck have I become?

"Although, I may talk a good game, I'm scared. I'm afraid of going to New York alone."

I was scared, too. I wanted to be honest and tell her the truth. Instead, I buried my secret, stifling the pain like a firewalker storming across hot coals. I screamed so loud but only in my brain.

She downed a massive shot of tequila. Then poured two more heavy hitters. "Chill, Saj! Seriously, I can't drink anymore."

"Hey, that's no fun. Where's my best friend? Where's Mr. Party-Guy?"

She put my hand on her chest. I pulled her close.

Next thing I knew, we were back at her house. I gazed at elegantly framed photographs of Mecca, Medina, and Jerusalem. I carefully avoided traipsing mud onto a well-worn prayer rug on the floor. "Where's your dad, Saj? Sure he's not coming back early?"

"Why?"

"I know he doesn't like me corrupting you. I don't wanna get you busted."

Saj glanced in the mirror.

"How come you always hide that dangerous body?"

"I like to, Codes. Sure, sometimes I'm a hypocrite but who cares. I think I look bomb with my hair in a hijab." She finally allowed herself to relax. She even let her hair down.

It was the first time I'd EVER seen her hair.

"Goddamn, you're hotter than whatever Victoria's keeping Secret!!"

"Time for body shots!" She slowed down her dance moves and sliced a juicy lime down to size. She seductively sprinkled salt across her neck. "C'mon, Codes. Lick it off. I know you want to."

I stared at her glistening butterscotch skin. "Remember what happened last time? You didn't speak to me for a month."

"No, Codes. YOU gave ME the silent treatment."

"I think that's pretty normal when you lose your virginity."

"Exactly! Two virgins, how the fuck were we supposed to know better? Worse part, I kept having nightmares my father found out and beat me. I'd wake up screaming."

I put my hand on her chest. "Hardest, but smartest decision I ever made—my entire life—was deciding that our relationship remain platonic."

"For thirteen years old, you were incredibly mature."

"Since I'm a gambler, I crunched the odds. Knowing most couples disintegrate, what are the chances we'd stay together forever? As far as our friendship is concerned, it was riskier to keep dating you."

"I thought you were the ultimate risk-taker?" She smiled strangely.

Was she oddly turned on by my refusal to have sex all these years?

"Since when does my bad boy follow rules?"

"No, our plan is perfect. We don't even think about hooking up—ever—until we get to New York!"

"What if you never make it? What if you don't get accepted?"

"Since when did you have such little faith?"

"C'mon, you knew exactly what was gonna happen when we made this pact."

"I won't break my oath to you. We're bigger than sex."

She planted her wet lips on mine.

"Wanna bet?"

present:

9:17 am

nervously twirled my Zippo between my fingers, like a magician practicing with a deck of cards. "Yo, I can't be the only dude you slept with."

"Doesn't every guy say that? What are you, a walking cliché?"

"Well, you've always been... well..."

"What? Say it!"

"Sometimes, you're..." I was entering shark-infested waters. "A little wild. Crazy. Impulsive."

"Oh, really? Just like you?"

I laughed. "Good one!"

Frustrated, she shook her head, "C'mon, can't we just figure this out? Together?"

"Chill, everything's gonna be cool. I'm at my best when the heat is on."

"Don't gimme your lame-ass rap."

"Hey!" A long-haired Security Guard stormed over. "You can't smoke here."

"Then I'm defying physics. It's a miracle."

"It's ok, we're leaving." Sajda stepped between us, snatching my cigarette and ashing it. "Look, I got a break at seven. Your white ass better be there."

"What? I'm a mutt."

"Ok, fine. Get your rainbow ass there."

CHAPTER FIVE

Road-Head

9:38 am

How the fuck did I knock up Sajda? Am I retarded? Don't I listen to Jay-Z and always squeeze on a rubber?

Extra tight?

An electric bus zipped me past the tiny Santa Barbara airport in Goleta onto the 225 highway. The fog hugged the coastline tighter than a thong.

I hopped off at Henry's Beach, ignoring the sandy steps leading to killer waves. I skated up a very steep Cliff Drive into Hope Ranch. Sweat poured down my back.

I kick-flipped to a stop.

Encased in a blanket of mist, the HOPE RANCH EQUESTRIAN CENTER resembled a palace fit for a Saudi Prince.

An armed guard circled a toll booth. I used the fog to camouflage my movements, sneaking around the side of the compound. I hopped a couple fences but the haze was so thick it rattled my brain. I double-checked my Apple Watch.

Did Emiliano really want to meet right here?

At the polo field?

Since when did he become Ralph Lauren?

Emiliano had never, ever, asked me to meet here. The fog temporarily rolled back, revealing a row of luxury boxes. Just beyond, huddled under a portable heater, were Eyez and Slim-Dre. Eyez, a black dude with a red mohawk, had a passion for prostitutes from broken homes.

"Lookie, lookie!" he snarled, letting his words linger like a foul snake. "Return of the Invisible Man!"

"A ghost!" Slim-Dre, a Mexican with jerry curls, announced. "Back from the dead!" He needed to lose a hundred pounds but no one's dared say it to his face for fear they'd be the next couple hundred pounds he ate.

They hovered ominously, surrounding me with their giant bodies. "What? Guys need a hug?" I said awkwardly. They were so close, I could smell the garlic-onion-jalapeno omelets they must've wolfed down for breakfast.

"Where's Emiliano?" I gazed across the field just as the curtain of fog rolled back in. I could hear the mighty waves of the Pacific smashing endlessly against the rocks.

"Go!" Eyez shoved me onto the field. "He's right in front of you."

I stumbled onto the wet grass, stepping right into a muddy crater. Goddamn, shouldn't have worn my new sneaks!

Although I couldn't see shit, I could hear Slim-Dre's BOOMING laugh. "Can't believe you made the boss wait!"

CLIP-CLOP. CLIP-CLOP. CLIP-CLOP.

Thundering hooves, louder than a locomotive, approached rapidly. I gasped terrified.

Is it a stampede?

A polo player burst through the mist.

His horse NEIGHED as he windmilled his mallet and SMACKED a bouncing ball.

WHOOSH!

The ball rocketed past my ear. Projectiles of grass and dirt landed in my eye. The sun finally cut through the June gloom.

I was shocked to realize I was standing right in the middle of a full-contact polo scrimmage.

WHACK!

Again, the ball whizzed past my dome.

I jumped aside as two jockeys CRASHED violently in front of me, almost pulling their mighty horses down.

A polo mallet shoved me hard in the back and I fell onto the grass.

My face landed in a deep puddle.

It felt like a disgusting tape worm crawled into my eye.

I turned and there was Emiliano, rearing his magnificent horse high into the sky. He looked more impressive than a Viking God.

"Stick with me, you can defy gravity," he said.

I stared, dusting myself off. *Kill me before I become his Ralph Lauren wanna-be.*

CHAPTER SIX

Emiliano's Law

9:44 am

A s Emiliano loosened his protective gear, Modesta, his awe-inspiring girlfriend, delivered him a Mint Julep full of crushed ice. He let the refreshing cocktail linger on his lips. Then, he kissed his girl-friend and I swear, Emiliano likes ice so damned much he kissed her with a full mouth of it.

I watched his hand slide gently down her hips to her tush—an ass that's launched a thousand wars. But her most striking fea-ture was her porcelain skin whiter than Madonna's.

Modesta was the kind of girl I thought about when it was late at night, I was lonely, and the only company I had was my calloused hand.

Emiliano wiped the sweat off his brow and took another big chug of his Mint Julep, followed by one more juicy French kiss for Modesta. "Only two sips for me," he said. "The rest is yours, *amor*. I don't wanna overdose on glucose before the second half. Besides, look at these deadbeats." He pointed across the field to a polo team wearing crimson. Brimming with Ivy League swagger, they looked like anything but deadbeats. "Think these Cito brats ever worked a real day in their lives? That's why I got the upper hand! Cause I've hustled all the way from the street corner to breeding, training, and racing horses."

I shuddered, never sure how to read his black eyes—darker than a shark's.

How the fuck did I make such a dumb mistake a year ago? How could I pick dealing drugs for this maniac over a scholarship at Oregon State?

"Baby," Emiliano turned to his Queen, "will you fetch my Ziploc of sports pills?"

She twirled the keys to his Rolls Royce Phantom before disappearing into the mist. I couldn't take my eyes off her.

"Fool," Emiliano snapped his fingers in my face. "Didn't you learn from 50 Cent? Don't be a sucker for love and chase hoes. Chase the paper and watch hoes chase you."

"Thanks, dad."

"Oh, right. I forgot your pathetic ass was adopted. Don't you think your real father deserves a beat down for passing on his loser genes?"

Ever wish you had a spiked metal bat?

"I bet you look in the mirror every day and ask—what the hell kind of mutt am I?"

"Hey, your skin is just as dark as mine."

"At least I know I'm Mexican. You don't even know what the fuck you are."

That hurt, because it was true. Despite the negativity, I tried to fly my happy flag high. "Your lady looks extra exquisite today, no disrespect."

"Blah, blah, blah. No small talk, homes."

"You sure? I got a whole bit about how long it's been since the last rain."

"Enough!" Emiliano shouted. "Tell me where the fuck you been all week, huh?!??"

"What you mean? I was surfing La Jolla."

"That's not what I heard. I heard you been here. Ducking me."

"Naw, you crazy? Sure your boy didn't just see Brad Pitt and get confused? Cause I would never, ever try to hide from you."

"You can't, Codes. My ancestors go back before the Spanish landed. Back when this whole city was a giant swamp of mosquitos. They tell me everything that goes down."

"Who? The mosquitos or..." I laughed nervously. "Maybe I should worry about you? You're the one gossiping with ghosts."

Emiliano pulled me around the corner, behind an electronic scoreboard. "I fronted you all that COKE, MOLLY, and KITTY! Where's the fucking twelve grand you owe me?!"

I turned into a STATUE—

And sure, I'm no fool, I know you're jumping to conclusions.

I'm not a scumbag just cause I lied to Sajda.

What was I supposed to say?

That I graduated to the next level on the muthafuckin' drug pyramid?

Hell, no!

You can't ever tell anybody like her anything about drug pyramids or next levels.

Cause to be honest, there's a huge difference between selling trees and cocaine.

One minute, you're with your buddies, you got a zipper, you're getting everyone nice and toasty, and next thing you know you're walking into a room and some crazy muthafuckin' Armenian dude's holding an AK-47 telling you to relax. 'Everything's gonna be ok.'

When every cell in your body is screaming that things are not O-MUTHAFUCKIN-K.

Crazy part—

I totally understood why Emiliano was so pissed.

He had every right to be.

And he deserved THE TRUTH.

a few
days ago:

Seven Falls, on a perfect sunny day, is a kickass spot to forget about life's bullshit. My buddies and I, in swim trunks, sat on huge boulders covered in ancient Indian rock art. I don't know if the Chumash were the first graffiti artists, but they were a peaceful tribe that didn't deserve to be massacred almost out of existence.

The boys and I smoked weed and drank beers. Dogfish 90 minute IPA. Heaviest beer in the world. Gets you drunk just gazing at the label.

Below was an awesome waterfall. On the nearby bank, some hippies picnicked and played guitar. We all stared at a beautiful girl swimming—naked—not a care in the world.

Couldn't have been better even if it was raining blunts.

Two FOREST RANGERS emerged—very interested in all our empty beer bottles.

Right then, I knew I was fucked.

The Rangers led us back toward the road. I eyed them carefully. When they weren't looking, I dropped my backpack into a flowering shrub below a soaring eucalyptus tree.

Back in the parking lot, the Rangers searched us thoroughly. I thanked Jesus, Zeus, even Saj's spiritual homey, Allah, for allowing me the opportunity to hide my drugs.

Frustrated, they insisted on writing us up.

"Underage drinking?" I was pissed. "C'mon, kids in Russia get a week in the gulag for not finishing their vodka. Besides, those bottles were already there."

The older Ranger sighed, "how'd you get alcohol on your breath?"

"That's just B.O. Happens every time I lick your momma's pussy."

The Ranger had a look I've seen too many times.

He wanted to beat the shit outta me.

that night:

snuck back into the forest with a flashlight. After a short hike, I spotted the towering Eucalyptus. *What the fuck? Where's my backpack?* I noticed bluepills scattered across the ground. I picked one up.

Fuck!

My Blue Batmans!!

A short distance away...

A ripped t-shirt.

SHIT!!

A frightening, unidentifiable sound grew louder around the bend.

Whoa! What's that?

It took me a moment to summon my courage. But, finally, I edged forward.

A huge black bear sat in a stream, tearing my backpack to shreds with his massive, gnarly teeth.

The bear pulled out my Ziploc full of white powder. Devastated, I watched him rip into my precious cocaine and MDMA, dumping it into the rushing water.

The bear roared as fluffy coke covered its giant mouth and nose. It sneezed loudly several times.

A fucking horrifying Yogi-Scarface hybrid.

CHAPTER SEVEN

Marco Polo

9:53 am

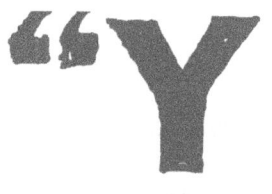ou've really taken this dog ate my homework shit to a whole new level." Emiliano stepped in my face. "And c'mon, if you're gonna spin a yarn, at least sprinkle in some comedy, huh? Throw in a virgin bride boning a dragon or something."

"All the girl-on-dragon porn I've seen, isn't it usually the dragon doing the fucking?"

I don't know if it was my All-Star delivery, or my billion-dollar grin, but Emiliano loved my joke so much he slapped me. His larger-than-life San Francisco World Series ring drew blood on my cheek.

"After all the cash I've piled up for you, you better not touch me again," I said, "Or—"

"Or what? You'll stick Cokey the Bear on me?" He laughed. "I'm a little sad you wanna go this way. You know, I had much higher hopes for you."

Before I could ask what those high hopes were, he tackled me.

He was grooming me to be his #2—but now—

I frantically tried to get on top but Emiliano had me pinned, choking my neck like an iron vice.

"Hey, what happened? Where's all your balls and sarcasm now?"

Emiliano pressed down so hard with his monstrous biceps I couldn't breathe.

My body flapped like a fish out of water.

And I thought working with Emiliano would be so easy.

Like busting a 360 kick-flip to Paradise.

CRACK!

Emiliano kicked me hard in the ribs.

"Either you get the 10K by six tonight, or I'll fuck you up so bad, you won't even be able to slang a Happy Meal at Mickey D's."

Emiliano jogged back to the polo field and mounted his horse. I watched the world sideways as the polo players raced, mallets in hand, to smack the ball into the goal. As they crushed it, I imagined myself being smashed to pieces by Emiliano.

Stop! Don't go down that track.

Remember what your therapist taught you? We choose our tracks. Now, make a big turn and go find some fresh powder in the trees.

I forced myself up and leafed through my wallet.

$187.

I reached in my backpack and pulled out a green envelope with giant letters scribbled across:

SAVE-DON' T SPEND!

Today is my rainy day. Time to break out the Ramen and tighten my belt! I tore open the envelope, adding a couple more c-notes. I didn't need to run the numbers on my calculator. I only had a lousy $387.

Still $11,613 short!

I nervously checked my pockets again, searching my socks thoroughly. Nice! I discovered a few extra crumpled twenties. I rifled through my back pocket. Nothing but lint and loose change.

How the hell am I gonna get 11K-plus by 6 PM?

CHAPTER EIGHT

Sex-Ed

9:58 am

I skated furiously past the wharf into an epic, carving turn onto State St. I ducked low as I narrowly avoided getting hit by a Police SUV, grabbing onto the back of a school bus. As I prayed not to get obliterated, the bus gave me an awesome ride into town.

Yeah, so not only did I lie to Sajda, I wasn't exactly honest with Emiliano, either.

Of course, the bear never snorted my blow!

I bagged that shit halfway to Saigon, amassing a small fortune. But, instead of being smart and responsible, I did what any other adopted idiot would've done—

I tried to locate my biological father. All I knew about my parents was what my adopted parents told me. That my mother died in a car accident only a few weeks after I was born.

"And what about my father? Did he die also?"

My foster parents didn't know. Nobody knew anything.

And that's what led me on this crazy, fucked-up quest to find my father.

Who was he?

And more important—

Who was I?

Here I was, desperate for clues, in the Adult Bookstore, Santa Barbara's first and only sex shop, staring at an army of vibrators, dildos, life-size sex dolls and never-ending selection of delicious lube.

That's what I needed big time for my first ever 69.

69—mutual oral sex—can be amazing—even mind-blowing—if you know what you're doing.

Which neither I nor Sajda did.

We sucked, slobbered, and drooled on each other for hours. Which I didn't mind cause Sajda's whole body tasted like an apple Jolly Rancher! Only setback was navigating through her full, wild pubic hair. I felt like I was swashbuckling Cortez, hacking my way through a dangerous Aztec territory to save my damsel in distress!

How do I find you? Magical, mysterious clit?

I had no clue what it even looked like. Do I just circle my tongue around her bush three times and toss in a few 'abracadabras?' Or should I just lick the top of the vaj? Or, better yet, how bout I just wiggle my tongue as deep as I can slither it in and pray for the best???

Or does the vagina possess a secret video game cheat code? I tried the infamous, UP-UP-DOWN-DOWN-LEFT-RIGHT-

LEFT-RIGHT-B-A. Nada. Just my tongue getting the biggest workout of its life!

Guess I gotta add this to the Cock Pushup routine.

I stared at a display of anal beads trying to figure out how on earth they were even supposed to be used.

Finally, my 'contact' arrived.

He was dressed like a bad spy in an Austin Powers movie. I couldn't tell if he had a fake beard, but he might as well have, because he looked like a goddamn Halloween prankster.

"Hopper, hey listen—"

"Sssshhhhh!" he refused to explain himself. Instead, he just signed me two letters. 'S' + 'B'. Then, he disappeared.

S + B?

What kinda crappy code is that?

I didn't have time to play his games. I texted him:

Stop taking this lame cloak & dagger nonsense so far, ok?

Just tell me where to meet you.

S + B?

Santa Barbara?

That doesn't make any fucking sense. We're already here? Did he make a mistake?

Did he actually mean, S + M???

As I headed for the door, a transvestite guard peeked through my bag. "Got any party favors, baby cakes?"

I shuddered, imagining for a second that this was Opposite Day and somehow, someway, I was attracted to trannies. But before I could slip too far down fantasy road, I spotted a roller-blader dude sipping a giant cookies and cream Frappuccino.

Duh, really??

CHAPTER NINE

Hop on Pop

10:09 am

I t was so completely obvious. Of course, S+B didn't stand for Santa Barbara. It stood for our national treasure, Starbucks. The joint was jam-packed with tourists excited to get it on for the Summer Solstice.

I spotted Hopper, holding down a table in the back all to himself.

I peeked at the poker game he was playing on his laptop.

"Only I know how to lose with pocket aces." Hopper was a short, wiry, Steve Buscemi kinda dude. Except he spent way too many hours jacked into the Matrix. Instead of early 30's, he looked like he was pushing 50. Maybe his diet of coffee, Red

Bull, and ginseng had finally caught up to his heart. Worst of all, he was starting to get twitchy.

"Didn't the Feds shut down online poker?" I asked.

"That's what makes it so much fun." Hopper laughed, brushing imaginary dirt off his shoulder. "Technically, I'm playing in Papua New Guinea."

Another reason I should've known Hopper wanted to meet me here in Starbucks, is that, unbeknownst to 99.9% of the world, your local neighborhood Starbucks has become quite the hotspot for cyber crime. Hackers love jacking in from their nearly-impossible-to-trace servers—and you can just sit, collecting all the beautiful keystrokes of everyone. Hopper tossed me a USB thumb-drive. "The entire Edward Snowden torrent. I'll let you borrow it, but you gotta promise to wipe it immediately after viewing."

"I, uh, I'd really love to dive into your cool discoveries. But today, I can't get caught up in your web of conspiracies. Actually, I just need my money back—"

"Easy with the C-Word, fool. Conspiracy connotes untruth. Why do you think Snowden defected?"

"I don't have time to get into this again."

A barista called out, "CODY! Gingerbread latte with organic skim?!!"

"Did you really order the extremely masculine 'gingerbread latte?' "

"They must've screwed my order."

I don't know why I felt the need to fib about a stupid latte. My adoptive mom always says that if you're willing to lie about the little stuff, you're more likely to lie about the big stuff. I couldn't agree more.

Eighteen years on this planet.

When do I not lie?

I grabbed my drink and hurried back to the table where Hopper was still immersed in his poker game.

Ok, no more small talk.

"Remember all that *dinero* I gave you to locate my biological father? Turns out I never should've given you a penny. Because now this crazy muthafucka wants to kill me for it. So I hate to ask. But I need it back RIGHT NOW! ALL TEN THOUSAND! Before this loco bastard drags my head down State Street."

"Whoa, wait, Cody, my brother." Suddenly, Hopper sounded very Asian, "Those Bitcoin you transferred me—I figured it was obvious. There are no refunds here. I wired all the money to a hacker named Sabu69 who guaranteed to find your old man."

Suddenly, I felt a ray of hope—I thought about meeting my real father—then I thought about Emiliano grinding me into salami.

"Sabu? Isn't that the dude from Anonymous who ratted out the other members of his crew? Fuck you doing collaborating with a rat?"

Hopper waved his arms in the air proudly after winning a big hand in online poker. "Man, you're just like every other orphan. Praying your real dad's a secret billionaire who will lift you into the clouds."

I flashed two crossed fingers. "Gotta have a dream, right, Hop?"

"Think he's still alive?"

"I've been waiting my whole life to find out. Usually, when someone asked if I ever wanted to locate my biological parents I always said, 'No, I took the hint when they abandoned me.' "

"You're being a half-empty guy overlooking countless incredible reunions. Like my brother's wife. She's adopted and the craziest thing happened. She became incredibly close with her boss. This older lady. They started going to lunch every single day. Soon, they were the bestest of besties. Someone randomly suggested they get a DNA test—BOOM—turns out the boss was her mother all along!"

Fucking Hopper, the world's greatest salesmen.

"What good is finding my dad if I'm dead? I need the money now."

"It's too late. Six PM tonight... Sabu will forward us a Dropbox account and passcode. Attached will be the intel."

To be honest, I was secretly glad he wouldn't give me a refund.

Fuck Emiliano.

He's not my dad.

CHAPTER TEN

Cloudy Piss

10:26 am

Now that the sun was in full force, all the tourists were ready to celebrate the Summer Solstice Parade—which began as a humble birthday party for a local mime—and mushroomed into the largest arts event in Santa Barbara County, drawing crowds of over 100,000 spectators from around the world. Every hotel was strained to the max. From the endless strawberry and lettuce patches of Ventura, all the way up the coast to wine country, Santa Ynez. Made famous in the movie *Sideways*.

Remember? The one where Paul Giamatti steals money from his mother.

I haven't sunk that low yet.

As I blasted back downtown, I was shocked to see so many cops—I felt like I had a big target painted on my back. Sure, Hopper put a gnarly thorn in my plans. I was hoping he was gonna return the 10K in full. But not to worry, I still got one more fat rabbit up my sleeve.

I pressed a button on my Apple Watch, dialing a number but it went straight to voicemail. "Christine! Hit me back, immediately! I got exactly what we talked about—just what you need—and no, it doesn't vibrate at three speeds."

I hung up, swerving behind a stretch limousine. I bent my knees back into bomber mode, relishing the wind on my cheeks. I'm most alive when my adrenaline's pumping full throttle as I'm dancing across the high-wire. No safety net. Just like my favorite movie, *Crank*. One false step and who knows, maybe I'd get that sweet dance with destiny... but no! I didn't have time to wax poetic about how I'd be remembered if I got smashed by a damn minivan. I just kept my eyes on the road, dangerously weaving and dodging, skating right past Death's Door.

I couldn't stop thinking about Christine. She was my GET OUT OF JAIL FREE CARD. Fingers crossed, if I sell her my entire stash of psilocybin mushrooms—I'd be back in the black and Emiliano will give me gold stars again.

Then, if I had anything leftover, I'd throw my own Summer Solstice keg party. Nothing like a fiesta to show Sajda I'm ready for fatherhood, right? And speaking of fatherhood—first step to being a great dad—make sure your DRUGS ARE WELL STASHED!

I quickly checked to make sure no one was looking. Or any security cameras.

Then, I dug frantically under a pink rose bush next to the County courthouse. I reached deep in my satchel, pulling out a baggie of pot, a Ziploc stuffed with various powdered-substances, and a small vial of bright red and orange pills. I buried my treasures in the hole. Satisfied, I covered it with a reddish-stone.

As I stood up, I froze.

Two motorcycle cops raced toward me.

But they zoomed past.

I breathed a sigh of relief as I pumped hard on my skate, getting a sweet little bomb as I circled around the courthouse. Glistening palm trees stretched toward the sun.

Although I didn't know jack about the town's history, I vaguely remembered learning that Santa Barbara was first discovered by Portuguese explorers in 1542 and that it was home to the oldest skeleton ever found in North America, The Arlington Springs Man, unearthed just 30 miles from downtown.

But that's all the crap you can pull up on Wikipedia. Let me tell you about the REAL FACTS you can't Google.

Because all that really matters is surf history. I'm talking Nordic Gods ripping waves by day and ruling the city at night. The biggest and baddest crew of all time, the "CITO RATS," first gained notoriety in the 70's. They "owned" every beach along the coast: Doro Dunes, Chicken Creek, Pigeon Ridge, Hammonds reef, Nuns, The Shooting Range, The Herb Estate and RKL—which spawned the seminal hardcore band: "RICH KIDS on L.S.D."

Before Oprah purchased her mega-mansion, the pad once belonged to an old Cito Rats family, the Shacklers, who used it properly—for legendary ragers of epic proportion.

I maneuvered into the Courthouse. All eyes on me, I felt like I was starring in a one-man Broadway show. The Vagina Monologues, starring yours truly, Cody Reese. Every cop, lawyer, bailiff, and district attorney had a front row seat and a rotten tomato aimed and ready. I jittered nervously through a metal detector. A beefy Security Guard eyed me like a nice delicious meatball sub.

I hope this Herbal Flush cleans my muthafuckin' piss. Cause if I pee dirty I'm going back inside. Back in the doghouse. Back in Hell.

Inside the Probation wing, I took a seat in the corner, away from the Mexican gang-bangers and black kids with 'NO HOPE' stickers plastered across their foreheads. I tried not to stare at an especially twitchy-tweaker who looked eager to teach me how to saw off a shotgun.

CHAPTER ELEVEN

Obey all Laws

10:31 am

Through a small slit in my bathroom stall, Earl Douglas had a perfect peephole to make sure I actually pissed into the cup.

"You like your drink shaken? Or stirred?"

But Earl wasn't in the mood. He was thirty-nine. Black, with a shiny bald head and intense eyes. He always wore dark rock 'n roll t-shirts and penned a popular hipster blog called, *The Black Rock Coalition.*

He took my urine, triple-checking its authenticity with a thermometer. He even smelled it. Satisfied, he led me back to his tiny, cramped, and terrible office. No window or ventilation. Just a small iron and a stack of shirts ready to press. I always wondered why he brought his ironing to work. But asking would be a little too damn personal.

My Apple Watch beamed with light. I checked the ID. CHRISTINE.

I was about to pick it up when suddenly I froze. It wouldn't exactly be kosher to QB a drug deal while I'm wining and dining my Probation Officer.

"Don't betray me hips," Earl groaned as he painfully slid back into his chair. "Not again."

He popped a few Ibuprofens and washed them down with a big swig of Rooibos tea. "You're taking something to beat the test. There was too much water in your piss."

"Then send it back to the kitchen. Thank God it's not illegal yet to work out. Makes you mad thirsty. You look like you could benefit from a few spinning classes to pump up your heart. Followed by a little Jazzercise. Then Yoga—cause you gotta stretch that asshole, right?"

"You know, you remind me of this loser Fritz that came through here." Earl shook his head in disgust. "Guy got a pissing-in-public ticket outside a bar July 4th. Never paid the fine. It doubled. Year later, a marshal served him with a summons. He skipped the court hearing. When stopped for a routine broken tail light, because of negligence, he had a warrant. The officers arrested Fritz on sight. Within months in jail, he got gang-raped and ended up with AIDS. Now Fritz's life is ruined. All over a two hundred and seventy dollar ticket."

"Luckily, I don't have to worry about that because I'll never piss on public property." I took a big sip of my Dr. Pepper. "I'll just go in this bottle right here."

"Two days ago we caught this kid tripping on acid near the square downtown. Kid was barely twelve. Said he got it from some guy who fit your description."

"Some guy with huge balls?"

"You're the kind of wise-ass falls into quicksand and pretends to enjoy it. But what you don't realize, I can mess up a million times and it doesn't matter. But the second I catch you clocking again—BOOM!—I'm gonna lock your sweet ass up for a long, long time."

CHAPTER TWELVE

Mad Paranoia

10:54 am

stumbled out of the courthouse a little shaken up. God-
dam what happened to following Biggie's Ten Crack
Commandments and watching the money pile up? Actually, maybe that's my problem. I got the wrong role models.

And why should I look up to Biggie?

Fat fuck barely outlived a fruit fly!

I jumped on my skate and made a wide, sweeping turn into
the parking lot. I hopped off next to the rose bush where I'd buried my stash.

A LOUD WHISTLE!

I froze in absolute terror. Two bicycle cops with wraparound shades peddled toward me.

I thanked the God of ganja, Jah, as the pigs hurried past.

Terrible spot to hide my drugs, huh?!?

This time, I scanned carefully in every direction to make sure no sneaky cops were lurking in the shadows. I even checked the sky for drones.

Goddamn Saj is right—

Dealing does make me fucking paranoid.

I'm always peeking over my shoulder—triple-checking every-one—cause maybe—just maybe—

They're a NARC.

CHAPTER THIRTEEN

Change of Heart

11:09 am

t had taken years for the prayers of Santa Barbara's Islamic Society to be answered. Finally, they had a mosque of their own. No one could have been more proud than Sajda's father, Masjid.

He stood in the sweltering heat, watching his daughter say goodbye to some of her old high school friends. All the young women wore beautiful, bright hijabs that Sajda had sewn for them by hand. Sajda blew everyone a big kiss before joining her father next to his Volvo.

"You'd tell me if something was wrong, wouldn't you?"

Sajda narrowed her eyes. "Of course, why would you even ask?"

Masjid pointed across the street—at me—anxiously waiting to cross over and join them. A barrage of traffic kept me at bay. I spotted my opening and pounced. Sajda gasped in horror as she watched me dash across six lanes of insanity.

Maybe I shouldn't have crossed illegally in front of Sajda's dad?

I couldn't even blame him for hating me. I know I'm not a Father's Day dream.

A UPS truck thundered past. I dove onto the sidewalk, miraculously avoided getting smashed like a bug.

Masjid stepped in front of his daughter, preventing me from even making eye contact with her. He glared through me like I was a pair of dirty pants and he couldn't decide if I needed dry cleaning or bleach.

"Really, Cody?" Sajda wasn't angry—more sad. "Can't this wait?"

"I'm sorry to interrupt your family and friends—but I'm afraid this is urgent."

"For once, Cody. I actually believe you speak a shred of truth." Masjid smiled. That same ear-to-ear grin as Sajda but his version was creepier, almost sinister. "Two minutes, cowboy."

COWBOY?!?

I bit my lip, finally taking a glance past Sajda. I couldn't have picked a worse moment to interrupt. The Islamic Society of Santa Barbara was having their annual event honoring the Solstice festival. A flood of African, Chechen, and Indonesian-American immigrants talked excitedly in their native tongues.

"Hurry, I'm timing you two!" Masjid warned.

Sajda didn't waste a second. She gripped my hand and we zoomed across the courtyard to the other side of the building.

Once her father was out of sight, I stopped, spewed an eruption of words. "Saj, I'm really, really... I mean, I wish I should've..."

But she covered my mouth, pulling me further around the corner. We hid behind an enormous eighteen-wheeler. "You trying to give my poor dad a heart attack? You know he forbids me from seeing you."

"Why does he despise me so much? What I ever do to him?"

"Oh, Codes, I don't know? Maybe, he wasn't so stoked you knocked up his daughter?"

"You told him?! Are you suicidal?"

"You are so gullible!"

I breathed a sigh of relief. "The reason I had to talk to you so urgently... I just wanted you to know how important—"

Suddenly, my throat felt drier than Death Valley. C'mon, pussy. Don't hesitate—just tell her exactly what you rehearsed a zillion times on the way over. "I'm sorry about earlier—I was just shocked."

Hey, that's not what you really wanted to say. C'mon, be honest. The apology is just an elaborate ruse. The real reason I'm here—

I NEED TO BORROW MONEY.

So c'mon, spill your guts!

Tell her the whole truth!

Maybe she'll feel so moved she'll sign over her entire financial aid check!

But, then, something happened—I don't know if it was the Force, or Obi Wan-Kenobi, or the sudden influx of tourists flooding in for Summer Solstice—I realized now was a terrible time to ask for a loan.

I reached in my wallet and pulled out a few crumpled bills. "Don't worry about anything, Saj. I'll pay for the whole enchilada, the casserole. Hell, I'll even pay for those spicy nachos you secretly pig out on when you think no one's watching."

"Are you saying you'll pay for an abortion? That's not your decision." She grew angry. "Who says I'm getting one?"

"You can't be fucking serious!?!"

"Look in the mirror, your parents didn't want you! Aren't you glad YOU didn't get aborted?"

"Of course I am. But we live in a different age. People are having fewer children—and later in life."

"You don't think for one second I'd let you be the father. You're still... you're still—"

"What?"

She danced around as if I was tossing firecrackers at her feet. "Not for one second would I let you near my kid!"

"That's cause with me as Dad, the little dude would come outta the womb smoking a blunt."

"If the procedure goes bad, I might never be able to get pregnant."

"You're perfectly healthy. Don't jinx yourself."

"I'm not deciding, Codes. I'm just weighing options. Which is a skill you need to learn, too."

"I refuse to stand here while you make the wrong decision. Dragging a little munchkin around would totally fuck up your dream."

"Don't you mean our dream?!? We were supposed to go to NY together! And just cause you have a kid doesn't mean you immediately forfeit your dreams. Look at J.K. Rowling."

Her words hit like a torpedo from a nuclear sub.

I kept blasting. "Look, in ten years, if you still haven't found a nice husband, I'll donate my sperm free of charge."

"The last woman on Earth wouldn't buy your sperm unless it ran her car! Besides, I can go to the sperm bank and find someone who's about to win the Nobel Prize. Harvard educated. One hundred and eighty IQ. Blue eyes. Blond hair. Six foot three."

"Great, get yourself a nice Nazi scientist."

"Now, Codes, if you had any balls, you would've gone to Oregon State last year. Accepted that more-than-generous scholarship."

Ouch!

"If I had any balls," I said, "I'd hop in a time machine, I'd make sure we never, ever had sex."

"So now I forced you to bone?"

"Did I or did I not try my hardest to keep the sex-pact intact?"

"Oh, I'm sorry I raped you. Why don't you skate off, hop into your imaginary time machine, and accept that Oregon State offer. Then, maybe, if you're really lucky—you can fix the biggest mistake of your life."

I grasped for a witty comeback but Saj had ripped the tongue out of my throat. I averted her laser eyes, spotting Earl—my probation officer. He glared at me from across the street, then whipped out an expensive digital camera.

SNAP-SNAP-SNAP.

But I wasn't Heidi Klum enjoying a fun photo shoot. I flipped Earl the bird and did a horrible moonwalk toward him. I really hammed it up big time for his camera. I channeled Michael Jackson, grabbing my nutsack a million times to make it triple-uncomfortable. "Stalk this, muthafucker."

"What's wrong with you?" Saj said. "Who are you even talking to??"

As Earl got into his squad car I noticed a huge blast of yellow paint on the side of his car.

The graffiti was mine—giant words seared across his driver-side doors like third-degree burns:

Ever feel like you just won the lottery?

But Earl's sinister glare turned my pleasure sour—fast.

As he slowly pulled into the street, Earl blew me a romantic kiss.

Damn, he's playing for keeps! Maybe I went too far tagging his ride?

Although I'm sure Earl wouldn't agree, I want to make sure you understand that I'm doing the world a huge service.

Until the world legalizes all recreational drugs, I supply the best you're ever gonna get. Because unlike your shady hookup, I'm not spiking my party favors with strychnine.

Or battery acid.

Seriously, if you could see the garbage most dealers sprinkle in with cocaine, molly, hash oil, and ecstasy... Even Charlie Sheen would shit a brick.

Why do you think I ever started slanging for Emiliano?

one year ago:

Emiliano had brought me camping at the Geronimo Trail Dude Ranch in Winston, New Mexico. For a week, we learned how to live off the land. Fishing. Hunting. Skinning game. Honestly, I don't think I ever wanna lasso my own dinner again, but I'll admit, it feels insanely good to get the fuck away from my phone for a few days. Besides all that hoity-toity shit, I'm probably still way too young to appreciate such a trip. My idea of a kick-ass vacation is raging down at the Ace or Roosevelt Pools in LA. *Just me, five girls, a bag full of powder, and a key to the penthouse!*

After Emiliano spent hours and hours seeing every single exhibit at the Los Alamos Atomic Museum, we hiked into the forest with our crossbows.

"Why fuck around with anything but the best?" I asked. "If Michael Jackson, Whitney Houston, or Phillip Seymour Hoffman woke up from the grave, what would I show them? They'd want some hard-core shit. Like they're the Devil getting stabbed in the eyeball with red-hot."

"You're missing the beauty of our business. There's no FDA crawling up our ass spot-testing our product. Nobody is ever gonna ask if our Ziploc bags leach toxic plastic chemicals. Or God forbid we're selling edibles loaded with gluten. So no, I don't think we should sell pure anything. Because we don't have to. Cutting blow and molly or any drug with Methylone or Pentedrone is DEALING 101. Why you think Scarface said never get high on your own supply?"

"Cause you'll snort the profit?"

"WRONG—the poison we spike it with—WILL KILL A MUTHA-FUCKA!"

"Exactly, that's why my clients desire a different experience. The last thing they want is to be wheeled out from Burning Man on a stretcher! There's a push to legalize drugs! Big names are leading the revolution! Howard Stern, Bill Maher, and Joe Rogan."

"Aren't all three of them comedians?"

"Didn't you say it's smart to diversify? The upscale Whole Foods crowd is dying for a clean buzz! I'm talking about people who drop twelve dollars on a cold-pressed cucumber-cayenne cleanser. Like Russell Simmons, that muthafucka spends sixty dollars a day on green smoothies!"

"Horizontal Integration?" Emiliano let the concept marinate in his brain like a shot of tequila. "I can buy into that. We can dominate both markets. My taxi drivers will handle the forty dollar cheap shit. You'll get the raw, uncut blow."

"We'll re-brand it VINTAGE 1980'S COCAINE."

Emiliano slapped me five. "And jack up the price 800%!!"

CHAPTER FOURTEEN

Slick Ricky

11:47 am

lthough, it was out of the way, I had to hit up the home base to pick up the rest of my party favors. I had an army of shrooms in a metal suitcase just like my man, Hunter S. Thompson, rolled in *Fear and Loathing in Las Vegas.*

Even though I stupidly wasted $10,000 looking for my real dad, if I can quickly move all this remaining dope, I'll be back in the black, baby!

I left my skate outside and headed towards a light emanating from the garage. My adoptive dad, Ricky, a thin man with a grey beard and round glasses, looked like a Merchant Marine sailor from the 1800's. He always covered his bald spot with a faded N.Y.P.D. cap. He loved to boast that he was once a boy in blue on the streets of Manhattan, but I knew the closest he got to the force was a night in jail for peddling Hustler magazines to neighborhood brats. Ricky poured some vodka into his mug, fired up his train set and gazed, glassy-eyed, as his train made a slow circle. I noticed a new, immaculately detailed train station in my father's mini-universe.

"My latest project," Ricky announced, proudly. "A real beaut, huh?"

I'm not here to talk choo-choos. "Hey, you ever think about having your own kids?"

Ricky looked at me, surprised. "Yeah, but your mom can't have kids. Or I can't. Hmm... I don't know. It's been so long I forget which one of us is infertile... Probably her, though."

I hesitated, grappling for the perfect words. Then, I spit it out like a big wad of Big League Chew. "Sajda's pregnant."

Ricky laughed. "Doesn't surprise me. She's black. She's gotta get pregnant before she's nineteen."

"Damn, dad, this ain't funny. And don't be racist, alright? She's pregnant cause of me."

Ricky reacted in the passive way he reacted to everything: by not reacting.

No head-nod. No sigh. Nothing!

I'm sure my real dad would have at least given me eye contact. Is that all I want? To be seen?

"D-d-d-did you hear what I said?"

Another long silence. Just when I thought I had to repeat myself for the third time, Ricky finally uttered. "So what you gonna do?"

"I was hoping to ask you."

"So ask."

"I just did!"

"No, you mentioned hoping to ask me."

I couldn't believe it. Wise guy's been taking care of me for thirteen years but never quits with the jokes. Just as I was leaving, Ricky finally said. "You can't support a kid. And we sure as hell don't need another hungry hippo here."

"Yeah, you're right, I don't want a kid. Shit, I'm still a kid myself."

"And there's nothing wrong with that!" Ricky grinned, "So what? Be a kid!"

"What if she doesn't want an abortion?"

Ricky took a drink and immersed himself in his trains, his teeny-tiny make-believe world. I sighed, stepping into the living room.

"Hey, can you teach me that awesome quarter trick, again?? Pleazzzzzzz???" Ashley, my ten-year-old sister, was one pudgy little bucket of energy. "I tried your trick for Sylvia and her friends but I kept messing up. They laughed—it sucked so so so so so bad! Please, teach me again?"

"THE KEY," I picked up a roll of scotch tape. "Don't let anyone see you put a tiny piece on the table."

I spread a bunch of quarters across the surface and lowered my voice for max effect. She loved when I gave her the whole charade. "LADIES and GENTLEMEN, I'm about to perform for you a very special magic trick. But first I need a unique, beautiful, smart and most important—"

"Skinny!"

"Skinny is over-valued! Way more important, I must find a WITTY assistant."

"Me! Me! Pick me!"

I pretended to interact with imaginary people in the audience. Finally, I gazed down at Ash and gave her a big high-five, pulling her closer to the table. "Alright, my super-mega-talented assistant. Would you please pick a coin from the table?"

Ashley grabbed a quarter. "Nineteen seventy-nine."

"Excellent! Now put that quarter on top of our tape." I tossed all the coins into my baseball hat and let Ashley shake them up. I closed my eyes, reaching my hand deep into the hat of coins. "ABRACADABRA!!"

Finally, I pulled one out, circling it through the air several times. "Why, my dear... could this be your lucky quarter?"

"Nineteen seventy-nine!" Ashley inspected the coin. "Where'd the tape go?"

"Scraped it off with my finger as I pulled it out of the hat."

Ashley grinned. "Now I'll be the coolest kid in school."

CHAPTER FIFTEEN

Thirsty &
Desperate

11:59 am

 disappeared into my Buddhist sanctuary a.k.a. my bed-
room. Tiny and completely dominated by a super-size
black and white poster of Mike Parsons riding a sixty-six
footer at Jaws Beach. *Maybe I should just lock the door
and never come out?*

I dialed Christine.

Again, straight to voicemail. "Where ya been sticking your head, you ostrich?!?"

I rifled through my contact list. If they had a goddamn phone, email, Facebook, Twitter, or Pulse, I hit 'em up:

Ball-breaking specials on Purple Playboys.

The real deal limited edition!

Google 'em! Only $9 each!!

And yes,

I'm still doing free deliveries.

I caught a glimpse of myself in the mirror.

Am I Irish? Ukrainian? Australian?

Probably I'm a goddamn Martian.

I called Hopper. My favorite hacker.

Why hasn't he called? Maybe he's full of shit and can't really find my father.

My call went straight to voicemail.

First Christine—now Hopper—were those two lovebirds on the lam together?

Damn! Stay Focused!

Or Emiliano's gonna slice me into sushi. I reached under a cabinet, unlocked my safe and pulled out an enormous Ziploc of drugs.

Even though I wasn't fully loaded, I still had the PARTY TRI-FECTA —

Coke,

MDMA,

and Ketamine.

Mix all three—WHOOSH—you'll be doing the K-WALK!

Speaking of K-Walk, my gay buddy Kevin replied to my mass text:

I'm at a party

at the most exclusive club in the world

that no one can get into—

MY DREAMS.

Alright, sleepy head, rock on with your bad self.

I got busy breaking down my molly and coke into smaller dos-es ready to slang. My crappy Dell laptop blasted a hip-hop clas-sic:

Finger on the shotgun.

Heaven.

Hell.

Prison.

Jail.

Dad's gonna taste 'em all—

But one.

A loud knock on the door disturbed my concentration.

Ashley called out. "Can I come in?"

"Gimme a break, ok sis? I'm late to meet my peeps."

"What peeps?" She was always asking mad questions, inves-tigating my every breath. And she had a better nose than a beagle. I don't know if she picked up a whiff of my shrooms or weed, but suddenly—

My mother barged in using her spare key.

"MOM?! WHAT THE FUCK!! DON'T YOU KNOCK?"

"Oh my..." Lauren's body went numb as she saw all my drugs on the table. To her, it must've looked like a monstrous amount, like I was the Wolf of Wall Street, sticking my face deep in a mountain of blow.

"This is my room!" I yelled. "My space! Get out!"

"No. NO. NO. NO! NO!" As if she could say no enough times, the whole situation would disappear. She took some deep breaths, faster, faster, and just when I thought she was hyper-ventilating, she said, almost calmly, "Don't worry. We can fix this." She grabbed my huge bag of drugs and stormed down the hallway.

I followed her into the BATHROOM—

She poured the bag—all the drugs I had—into the toilet! "STOP!! You don't understand, Mom! I still have to pay for this!"

I ripped the bag from her, accidentally body-checking her into the tub. Her head slammed onto the porcelain with a loud thud. Horrified, I couldn't believe what I had done. Blood oozed down the back of her head.

"Shit, Mom. I'm really, really sorry." I tried to help but she moved away. I could literally see the lifetime of worries flashing through her brain.

How could I be the same little angel she adopted?

All I knew, staring at her bleeding, it was impossible to justify any decision I'd made up to this point.

"Our dream was always to adopt a kid. You were so good when you were young—"

"And I still am good! I got a strict code you couldn't possibly understand! Besides, where do you think that money came from that saved Ashley's life? Did you really believe I found it under our avocado tree?"

Ashamed, she bowed her head.

"Oh, I get your M.O. So, it's ok to take drug money when one of us is dying and needs expensive, emergency surgery. You sure took the cash then, didn't you, Mom?"

"Go. Get out!"

"I was about to—"

"No, you don't get it. Pack your bags. You're never stepping foot in my house, again."

CHAPTER SIXTEEN

Adios, Muthafucka

12:17 pm

uckily, I grabbed my Ziploc of precious powders before my mom was able to flush the majority of it
down the drain. No insurance for lost dope. Hey,
that's not a bad idea! I should invent an app—selling
insurance for lost drugs. I'll make millions and retire
on a yacht in Antigua.

I ashed a cigarette underneath a tree house in the front yard
of my house. So many good times here. Not only could this fort

ward off invaders, but it was the site of my first BJ. One day, families from Vermont would rent cars from LAX to visit this historic spot.

I reached behind the tree house, into some dense ivy. I felt a rat scurry past my hand, but I didn't have time to worry about rodents. Inside a garbage bag, I pulled out a large cooler. I checked the seal. It looked fine except for a tiny crack.

I flipped open the lid and was greeted with the most beautiful sight:

FIVE POUNDS OF MAGIC MUSHROOMS.

Just in time for the SUMMER SOLSTICE.

Even if Christine doesn't want these beauties, I can find plenty of other wealthy hippies eager to fry balls.

I turned to the street, soaking up the neighborhood one last time: rusty, dented cars parked along the cracked sidewalk. The faint sound of a Mariachi band played at a fiesta next door. I could smell the cheesy tamales getting cracked out of their shells as a pimped-out low-rider rolled by, cranking lame-brain Raggaeton to ear-splitting levels.

"You crying?"

Ashley walked up behind me.

I quickly rubbed my eyes. "It's just... allergies."

"Sorry I got you in trouble."

"Don't be. I'm like Godzilla. Wherever I go, I leave a wake of destruction."

"You know what happens to Godzilla at the end of the movie, right?"

I hesitated, "He marries the princess?"

"Duh, that's Super Mario." She held out a ball of rolled-up newspaper.

"That supposed to be a present?"

"For when you're skating. This way, even if you can't afford to pay your cellphone bill or your battery dies."

I peeled back the silver wrapping, revealing an antique copper compass. "Wait a second, I appreciate the gesture, but you can't give this to me. It's the only thing your real dad ever gave you. Forget it."

"Now, no matter what, Codes. You can always find me. No matter what, right?"

I hugged her tight and couldn't let go.

Ashley's the only person I've really got in this crummy world.

CHAPTER SEVENTEEN

Panty Party

12:59 pm

I roared on my board past cheap taco stands and run-down laundromats. Thugs with bandanas and imitation shades tossed dice on the corner, shooting the shit, getting faded on this blisteringly hot Summer Solstice day.

After passing endless BBQ's, *piñatas,* and barrels of Pacifico, I kick-flipped to a stop next to a modest house with thick iron bars protecting the windows.

"CHRISTINE! Open up, baby! C'mon!" I banged furiously on the door. "Hey, it's mad important!"

Silence.

What if she's on holiday?

I fought the urge to kick in the door.

For real, goddamnit!

What if she's visiting a relative?

Do I know ANYBODY else who would buy my Costco-sized bag of shrooms?

I threw my skate onto the ground and half-heartedly jumped on, attempting to grind a bench. But skating punishes you for laziness. I stacked hard onto the pavement.

"ROOKIE!" A voice shouted. "Maybe you need some training wheels?"

I quickly brushed myself off. "Aren't you a sight for my Chinese eyes!"

"Homey, what a night!" Christine growled, standing in her doorway. She had long dreadlocks like a Burning Man rasta-babe. "I taught two beauties Kundalini tantric breathing. I must've made them both orgasm fifteen times!"

"Fifteen orgasms?!? That's terrible! You must be mad sore."

Now I understand why her phone was off all morning. *I wouldn't have picked up till next week.*

"How many times I gotta school you, boy? Women aren't built in a limited way like you dudes. We don't just blast a load and pass out. We can orgasm infinitely."

"How you EVER get out of bed?"

"I didn't, Codes, the last twenty-four hours I was locked in my room with two gymnasts. I just got two pairs of new handcuffs—imagine the possibilities."

I pushed past Christine and invited myself into her house. Christine's pad had the best vibe in the world. I don't know if it was the incense or all the candles, but the minute you strolled in, you couldn't help but want to slip off your shoes and get cozy. She had a room dedicated to brewing delicious moonshine. Her apple-pie-flavored-shine was flying off the local shelves. Her plan was to find an investor and market worldwide—like Tito's vodka. Across the wall, a projector beamed music videos, nature documentaries, and of course, trippy films about astronomy.

An insanely-attractive naked woman hopped out of the bathroom and scurried into a bedroom.

Christine's running a turnstile, isn't she?

"So," Christine said, "got those Oregon boomers from the psychedelic church?"

"Blue Angels," I whipped out the metal box of mushrooms. The caps and stems all looked like tentacles ripping each other apart. "Got a killer high. No roller coaster ride. Just eat one of these dense-ass caps and you will be flipping!!!"

"I'm getting moist!" Christine packed some in a pipe and took a rip.

"Wow! You're gonna fry already? It's barely past noon."

"Just a little something to make the colors pop."

She forced me to take a few hits of the shroom pipe too. Even though I didn't want to. Satisfied, she counted a stack of hundred dollar bills and slammed them on the table. "Five pounds? Nine grand?"

I stared at the money and hoped Christine didn't notice, but my mouth started watering.

Oh, yeah, baby.

Gonna pay back Emiliano! No more hiding in the bushes avoiding his calls.

"Hey, man!" Christine snapped. "WHAT THE HELL?!? This shit's all moldy!"

"Fuck you talking 'bout mold? Where? Show me!"

"Dude, right there! All kinds of nasty white shit on the stems. You blind or something?"

"No, those are shroom crystals."

"Shroom crystals?! You moron, only weed has crystals. Check it, fool. The microscope is better than a lie detector test."

She passed me a magnifier. I examined the shrooms carefully. "Fucking A! My case had a tiny crack! The moisture must've gotten in when it rained the other night."

"You ever gonna learn some damn RESPONSIBILITY?! Aren't you too fucking old to be pulling off this teenage crap? You gotta love and treat your magic mushies like a delicate pet!"

*Are you as sick of that **R-WORD** as I am?*

"Ok, you're right, I should've double-checked the drugs were in the box with the lid tight! So what, uh, no problem... How about I give you a wholesale price on some Rock Star White and you'll flip it like a pro?"

"I look like a fucking cokehead to you?"

"Chill, dude. Don't act like you ain't never blasted a bump," I said. "How about some K? You wanna kiss the Kitty Kat? And I also got these insane Blue Batman's and Purple Playboys you want those? You take these off my hands and I guarantee, you'll have every chick in SB waiting in line to suck your big black dick."

"Don't you realize your lame attempts to butter me up don't work?"

"Please, man. C'mon. Help." My iron mask of cool finally melting away. "Emiliano's gonna jack my ass up. I owe him $12,000! I spent all the cash on this crazy hacker looking for my dad. I don't even know if he's alive or dead. I'm so fucked. And you're right. You always told me to think before I act, and I should've skipped all the B.S. and just asked you for a loan."

"First you trick me? Then you have the balls to ask for a loan?! Hell's wrong with you, boy?" Christine yanked her money off the table. "I look like Goldman Sachs?"

I searched for a lifeline but I was sinking faster than the Titanic.

Christine, furious, shook her head. She was devastated that I, her former pupil, had sunk so low. "I hope Emiliano washes your mouth with turpentine cause you need way more than just a spanking."

CHAPTER EIGHTEEN

Butt-crack Benito

2:37 pm

o Christine was an epic fail. But I didn't have time to cry in my panties. I ripped past the famous Morton Bay Fig at the train station. CHOOO-CHOOO. An Amtrak loaded with passengers eased down the tracks toward Mexico.

Maybe I should hop on? Not worry about babies, a $12,000 debt or a vindictive Probation Officer out to fry my ass.

I was determined, however, to go down swinging.

I skated hard through the Summer Solstice traffic, snaking my way to the Fiesta Five movie theatre. An old, run-down dump.

The rest of the city had been revamped to get tourists spending max bucks and this relic was a throwback to the era of grainy film, tiny screens and crappy sound. So no one came for the films—they came for the parking lot. It had the best views in town and was perfect for roasting bowls, drinking 40's, and making out with a little darling.

An ambulance swooped in, honking three times.

"How long you trapped working?" I high-fived the EMT driver, Butt-Crack Benito, a tall Argentinian with a nasty scar across his cheek.

"Why? You crazy muthafuckas partying again?" Even though he was only twenty-three, you could already tell Benito missed being wild and out-of-control. "You betta savor every second, cause you ain't gonna be eighteen fucking jailbait forever."

"Jealous?" I hopped into the passenger seat. Benito double-checked his funds and handed me a large stack of twenties. With a five on top instead of a cherry.

I fanned out the bills. $825. I passed him a Ziploc stuffed with blue and purple pills. The best ecstasy in the game—BLUE BATMANS and PURPLE PLAYBOYS. "Ready to roll so hard, your face will feel like it's melting off?"

"Yo, so gimme the low on Ernie? How the fuck he O.D.?"

"Can you keep a secret?" I leaned close. "He's dead because he didn't get his dope from me."

"Why? Doesn't he know you only rock that Vanna-White-white? And most important, that you always test drive your product?"

"Exactly! Every drug has to meet my STAMP OF APPROVAL. The same exact thing the FDA does with food. It's gotta be ver-ified. If you're buying ground beef, someone needs to make sure it's not fake beef from China made of rat guts. Or, even worse, small canines. That night Ernie was too cheap to buy my sassafras. Guy asked me for a discount and I just laughed. Next thing, I see him convulsing on the dirt."

"Sure," I whispered. "I could've cut him a deal and given him one stupid little bag for cost. All he wanted was some kick-ass chemicals to send him on the ride of his life!"

"So Ernie died because he was too cheap to fork over a lousy $40?!?"

"Fuck."

Maybe I should've given him a freebie?

CHAPTER NINETEEN

Candy for Strangers

2:51 pm

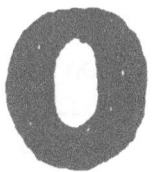nly $825 in the can! *Time to ratchet the old Cody charm into high gear and make magic!*
For the first time all day, I hit up the Solstice Parade. An exhilarating, psychedelic blend of danc-

ers, drumming, scary puppets ripped from a Tim Burton night-mare, and 'barely-legal' dancers happily showing off way more than their belly-buttons.

Talk about a double-edged sword.

Sure, the festivities brought an armada of cops. But it also lured a rowdy crowd of ragers ready to rattle and roll. Yeah, it was dangerous, and I usually NEVER, EVER SOLD TO STRANGERS, but today I had to break every rule. So I sliced and diced the sacks of special K, blow, and molly like a veteran Sam-urai—till I only had one bag left.

Fuck man, I'm so good at this. But Sajda thinks I'm wasting all my talent. I wish I had as much faith in my art as I do in my ability to push drugs.

"Think this town appreciates your graffiti skills?" She had told me yesterday. "New York! Remember our promise?!"

I tried to push Sajda outta my brain—but thinking about her just made me want to create. I was sick of being Emiliano's monkey. I busted out an industrial marker and practiced a new tagging style on a bus bench.

Sajda was right—

I did want to take on the world using my art skills.

And there was no way I could do that by staying in SB.

I needed someone to push me to the next level.

That's why I needed to go to New York. With Sajda sitting on my good shoulder, whispering that I can do it. Fighting all the demons on the other shoulder telling me I can't.

Instead, here I was, getting caught up in the monotony of dealing. Because most of the time, you're not popping bottles with models or dropping mollies on tongues—you're waiting in a parking lot staring down Father Time.

TICK-TOCK.

A MOTORCYCLE COP ripped past.

I ducked my head and tried to blend in with the crowd on State St. A group of Brazilian belly-dancers gyrated around a rainbow float. A marching band broke into a powerful drum solo.

A PAC MAN float trailed behind, ready to gobble everyone up. POLICE RADIOS crackled behind my ear.

I barely avoided getting crushed by three police on Segways. They zigged and zagged in a circle around me.

Are all these cops after me?

Am I surrounded?

Outside the always-packed Coffee Bean & Tea Leaf, surrounded by a thick posse of cops, stood Earl, my probation officer, sipping a blended latte and looking too pleased with himself.

Earl nudged a fellow officer, pointing at me.

Suddenly, all the cops around him turned their focus to me.

I imagined they had x-ray vision and could see right through my bag packed with dope.

I couldn't help but walk weird.

Or was I walking normal?

Goddamnit, get a hold of yourself!

But, dude, get real—

HE JUST POINTED YOU OUT TO ALL HIS COP BUDS!

I ducked back into the crowd. Hurried around a corner. Almost ran into—

"What the hell are you doing here?" I stared, speechless.

Emiliano towered over me. "What the hell are you doing here?"

There a fucking echo in here?

"You never answered my question, Codes."

"Actually, I'm really glad I ran into you. Things are really cooking. You wouldn't believe how many chemicals are flying off the shelves—everyone here wants to expand their mind!"

"There's only one thing in this world I want to expand."

"Your dick?"

"Don't you ever think with something you don't piss out of?"

"Speaking of pissed. I got something to cheer your grumpy ass up. I've called all my connects. Hustled and flowed like a muthafucka. Sold all my inventory—"

I awkwardly handed him a humongous wad of bills. "Here's $2,500."

Unfortunately, a huge blast of wind blew a few bills into the street!

A group of kids, dressed as giant M&M's in the parade, grabbed all the free money.

"This is barely one-fifth of what you owe. What were you wasting the last couple hours doing? Waiting till the last second to squeeze some miracle out of your ass?"

"Exactly," I checked my watch. "Any moment now I'm due to start shitting money."

Emilano stared with such terrifying focus I thought for sure he was going to project a beam of ruby-colored concussive force from his eyes and melt me.

No, Emiliano isn't a lame-ass Marvel X-Men.

He's Hannibal Lecter mashed-up with Steve Jobs.

A

Thirsty

Hungry

Terrible task-master.

Always *more more more.*

"I just need a couple more days to call my fleet back to port. Please, I beg you. Give me an extension."

"What are you? Greece?"

"Greece?"

"Do I have no tits and an iron smile?"

I laughed. "Yeah, why."

"You really think I'm Angela Merkel? That just because I'm the leader of Germany, the economic powerhouse of E.U., that I'm gonna bail you out and wipe your ass every time you cry?"

"Emiliano, please. Listen to me. I've never been late on a payment once. Right? So what the fuck? And you don't give a shit about nine thousand, five hundred bucks. You gave my parents thirty-five grand when my sister needed emergency heart-valve surgery."

"I don't know what you're talking about. I never gave her a penny. Besides, didn't you tell me a mysterious man handed your dad a garbage bag stuffed with cash?"

I looked into Emiliano's eyes and tried to reach beyond the darkness. But he had less emotion than a mug shot.

"We both know it was one of your guys because…. well, who else could it be?"

He wouldn't budge.

I shook my head.

Why won't he admit he saved my sister's life?!

Emiliano's girlfriend returned with a giant frozen margarita. She put her arm around him. "When we going back to Costa Rica?"

"Pronto, bonicisma! Pronto." Emiliano pinched me on the cheeks.

Like a goddamn, baby.

I fought the urge to smack him.

"Don't give up pounding the pavement, right?" he whispered. "Maybe you'll even surprise yourself."

CHAPTER TWENTY

Insane in the Membrane

3:14 pm

I blasted through the open gates of a Cito mansion. Even though it was a sprawling estate, it looked run-down, almost deserted, like it was a vacation home for the Addams Family.

I 360-flipped to a stop.

A shrill voice boomed from upstairs.

The front door was ajar. I cruised in, climbing up a massive staircase past a crystal chandelier.

If anybody in Cito could give me nine grand on the spot, it was Dane.

And there he was: a nineteen year old with bigger muscles than The Rock, breaking through a wood-paneled door like it was made of paper. I tried to pull him back.

"You might be my BFF, Codes. But you don't understand my mom." Dane tossed me aside with barely a flick of his powerful wrists. A few more karate chops and he busted the door off its hinges.

"Don't come in! I'm working!" Dane's mom, Francine, shouted inside.

"I know you're spying again, mom." Dane marched into her office. "I found the video camera you hid in my room."

"You treat this place worse than an hourly motel. Every night you drag tramps over. All night I hear you—"

"Stop watching me have sex! Or, do you enjoy it? Does it get you off? You're disgusting, Mom."

"No, you are! Yesterday, I counted. You pleased yourself six times!"

I laughed loudly. I know I'm a piece of garbage for laughing at my friends' sex habits, but imagining Francine spying on her son while he greased his monkey was too much. Dane was so embarrassed his face turned cherry red. He picked up her prehistoric Compaq desktop, angrily ripping all the cables from the back.

"Stop! That's delicate!"

Dane opened the window and chucked out her computer. It landed with a fireworks of gizmos, screws, and wires. "Now, maybe you won't be such a Peeping Tom. Hey, look at me. Did you forget to take your medicine today? Again?"

Dane pulled her into the bathroom. She fought, wriggling desperately to break free of his grip. "Be strong!" Dane commanded. "C'mon, I hate doing this!" He pried open her mouth, held her nose closed, and forced her to drink the horrible brown medicine. She coughed some up.

I couldn't look away. I felt so bad for her. Better to be dead already, right

CHAPTER TWENTY-ONE

Skate &

Destroy

3:49 pm

 on't be lazy, Codes! We'll find mom's secret stash," Dane said. "She was just at the bank."
Soon as I told Dane I was short $9,500, he offered to let me steal from his mom.

Talk about 'best man' material, right?

We ripped through his dilapidated mansion, searching under every pillow, cabinet, and couch for a hidden cache. But all we found were unopened bills from the Montecito Water district, Southern California Edison, and a host of credit card companies looking to suck his mother dry.

As I tip-toed into the living room, I started to feel sick. This damn room always made me feel weird. I wondered if it was the all-white furniture. Even the brass doorknobs were painted over. Only thing not pure white was an ivory grand piano. I don't know if it was those damn shrooms I smoked with Christine, but I could feel the eyes on the oil paintings glaring at me.

"Your mom take a hit in the stock market?"

"You're joking, right?"

"What'd she do with all her awesome furniture? Remember that insane marble statue of the Tibetan elephant god?"

"Sold. Everything. To pay off her medical debt. Sold a dozen silver forks and spoons on eBay and she's been living off it for almost an entire year. Only eats one can of tuna per day. And she is so scared, she never turns on the lights or air conditioning."

"C'mon, help me brainstorm a way outta this mess. Then we'll start a charity for your mom."

"You only need nine thousand, five hundred? And we got two hours? That's nothing for a couple of Einstein's like us. I know... we'll jack an ATM!"

"Make that one Einstein and one Homer Simpson. How the hell could we even do it?"

"Easy, chain it to my truck and drive it the fuck outta 7-Eleven." Dane led me into his mother's bathroom. Since I could hear her only a room away, snoring deeply in her bed, I felt kinda guilty rummaging through her medicine cabinets. Underneath jars of long-expired vitamins, I pulled out a vial of pink pills. "Cyanide? Your mom planning on murdering you?"

"I told you, stupid." Dane snatched the vial, putting it back on the shelf. "My mom's got Cervical Cancer. Worst part... sometimes she thinks she's gonna have to pull her own plug."

"Suicide? Not your mom, she's one tough *bruja!*"

"Glad I can always count on my best bud to call my cancer-stricken mom a witch. But seriously, she's unstable. That's why I carry this twenty-four, seven." Dane reached into his wallet, struggled with a tiny zipper, and revealed a monstrous blue pill. "This antidote gives me one minute, maybe two, to save her life."

I read the side-effects. "Nausea, dehydration, and blue skin."

"Blue skin? Heavy shit."

I could tell Dane didn't wanna harp on his dying mother.

He bounced restlessly from room to room.

In the basement he busted out a furious barrage of pull-ups. One, two, three... ten... twenty... His bloodshot eyes bulged madly as he passed fifty. He flexed his biceps. "I'm ready, muthafuck-er. In case the cyborgs take over when the Singularity hits."

I wanted to tell him he sounded like a half-a-maniac, but instead, I slapped him on the back. "Glad to have you back home in Paradise."

"I've learned there's more to this world than bikinis, beer, and gnar-gnar waves. When you gonna join me in enlightenment, bro?" He guzzled a giant protein shake. "Chasing Boko Haram in Africa, I was really making a difference. Not only are doped-up child soldiers armed only with spears sent wave after wave into machine-gun fire—but let's talk about shit! These poor bastards, forget about toilets and plumbing, they can't even afford a decent porta-potty! Everyone just squats at the beach, drops a fat deuce, and prays a tapeworm doesn't bite their asshole."

"You still haven't told me why you're home two years early. Didn't that judge force you to sign a four-year commitment?"

I knew there was some ugly secret he wasn't telling me.

I could smell it.

Dane was a trouble magnet—the kind of bastard who breaks a mirror just for kicks.

"Aren't you over this town, Codes? How many times can you bone a college slut behind an Eos dumpster?"

"I will not front. I love everything about a new girl... the excitement, the smell, the uncertainty will always rattle my brain!"

"You really need to get the fuck out, bro. There's something in the air or water here—you just wanna do stupid shit and get tossed in jail."

"Dude, you weren't really in Nigeria." I noticed some medals in an open drawer and picked one up. "Bet you ordered these on eBay!"

Enraged, Dane grabbed me. "Eat them, fool!" Dane twisted my arm behind my back, shoving my face into the drawer. "You don't believe they're real? Why don't you taste the metal and find out?"

"WHOA! Easy, doggy. I was just fucking with you! Lemme go!"

"You wouldn't last a second in Africa." Dane relaxed his iron grip. He grabbed his wallet and ripped out all the cash—a thick pile—and held it out to me. "Wish it was more. But some jackass forgot to pave the Nairobi roads with gold."

Grateful, I leafed through it.

Although it looked like a lot—

I quickly realized it was mostly small bills, less than $200 total. "Even with your extreme generosity, Emiliano's still gonna chew my ass up."

"Then there's only one option. We take him out."

"Chill, Rambo. This ain't Mogadishu. Besides, his sister's in the Sinaloa cartel. She'll cook us alive. Turn us into Carne Asada!"

"Dumb-ass, how many millions of Uncle Sam's bucks have gone into training me?" Dane pointed to the Special Forces tattoo on his bicep. "Make it look like Emiliano went on a nice, relaxing vacation at the bottom of the Bermuda Triangle."

"You're insane. Remember in Junior High when you got expelled for beating up that principal who was always making your life a living hell?"

"Codes, my shrink told me it's not constructive to dwell in the past." Dane smiled mysteriously, reaching under the couch and pulling out an AR-1 5 assault rifle. "But I'll admit, beating up Principal Whitfield was one of my finest moments. Actually, I'm touched you remember."

I eyed the massive gun nervously. "Why the fuck you need that?"

"You know why you came here so stop playing dumb!" Dane checked the clip, making sure it was loaded and ready for battle.

He snapped off the safety and aimed the gun.

BOOM.

The TV screen shattered into a million pieces.

CHAPTER TWENTY-TWO

North Side

4:08 pm

The wind blasted through my hair as Dane's truck rumbled up the winding hills of Montecito. He had this whacked out idea that he could get all the money I needed from some MILF he had been fucking before he joined the service.

Only problem—

She wasn't answering his texts.

Still, she often went incommunicado, so he thought it was worth going to her house, which unfortunately was way up at the top of Hot Springs Road, right near Jeff Bridge's pad.

At this point, I had no other choice.

I gazed at an elementary school that rivaled the splendor of an Ivy League campus. Maseratis, Ferraris and Bentleys blasted past.

Cito's such a rich town, even the homeless women are hot.

"Man, I just wanna live THE GOOD LIFE FOREVER!" I yelled out the window as we blasted past old Mount Carmel Church. "How come we haven't started that skate company we're always dreaming about? Fuck we waiting for? Someone to smash a board on our heads?"

"You're a half-way decent salesmen when you're not higher than the Goodyear Blimp."

"What will you do? Work security?"

"Sure, I'll beat up the customers if they don't buy nothing."

I laughed, "We'll set up headquarters in Bali, rip gnar-gnar waves and toke doja on pristine beaches of cocaine-white sand. The sweet, sexy jungle full of monkeys climbing on our backs while we drink Bintangs and slam every Australian tourist!"

"TO THE DREAM!" we roared in unison. Dane and I, two fatherless bastards, were one sick and twisted family.

"What's the dealio with Saj? I was gone over two years—almost killed—and she won't even call me back. I thought we were friends."

I kept thinking about a night, years ago, when everyone played spin-the-bottle at the cemetery. I'll never be able to burn away the image of Dane French-kissing Sajda. Even though he's my best friend and it was just kissing—it still makes me nauseous.

"Hey, you love magic. Bet one flash of her magnetic smile and POOF—ten thousand dollars will rain down."

"As if. Get real—we don't wanna waste her time. She works, you know. Has a real job."

"While I was gone, did you guys ever hook up?"

I anxiously twirled my Zippo.

"C'mon, we both know you've had a King Kong boner for her since T-ball."

All I wanted to do was TELL THE TRUTH—

OF COURSE I FANTASIZED ABOUT SAJDA!

"I'm about to get my head blown off," I said, "and all you can think about is where I stick my prick?"

My watch beeped. An email from Hopper. I didn't want Dane to see who it was so I reached into my backpack, tilting away from Dane.

But Dane didn't wanna cooperate. "Who's that? Tonight's Tinder date?"

I leaned toward the window, away from his prying eyes. I opened Hopper's email. It read:

'CHECK YOUR VOICEMAIL!!'

Fucking Hopper. More hoops than the damn Olympics.

I swiped over to my voicemail. I don't remember my phone vibrating but there it was. A missed call from Hopper at 4:02 PM.

I eagerly pushed play. Nothing but—

STATIC—a river of HISS.

What the fuck? $10,000 and the guy can't even leave an audible message. Paranoid nut could've put everything in the stupid email!

I wanted to scream. But I was too embarrassed to tell Dane the truth about where I spent the money I owed Emiliano.

I blasted Hopper with a barrage of text messages:

Where the fuck are you?

Sup with your piece-of-shit phone you cheap bastard?!

Any word on my father? That bastard still alive?

Then I blew up his twitter page:

Call me, you sexy beast! I couldn't hear your voicemail!

Is your phone working?

HEEEEELLOOOOO!!??!!!

YOU ALIVE?!??!!?

I stopped, knowing that I'd gone too far. If I were him, I would probably ignore me, too.

I stumbled onto his Instagram page and was shocked to see his latest post. A selfie of Hopper grinning in front of the shadiest massage parlor in the city.

Goddamn, that asshole!

Instead of helping me—

He's getting his chain jerked!

OK, calm down. Don't always assume the worst. I couldn't hear his message. Perhaps it wasn't important. Otherwise, he wouldn't be getting a rub down?

Would he?

He promised me the info by six PM. Exact same time I gotta report to Emiliano.

Talk about a clusterfuck.

My Apple Watch beeped. Incoming text.

Thank, God!

Better be Hopper.

I sighed in frustration. It was only Ricky, my adoptive father:

Mom told me what she found.

Not only have you ruined my Solstice—

but we need to talk.

Before I could press delete—

A monstrous 7.2 liter v12 engine roared behind Dane's truck:

THE RAMBO-LAMBO

A Lamborghini beloved by billionaires around the globe because it was the only four-wheel drive ever built by the Italian firm. The beast was crammed full of angry teenagers laughing and screaming. Not only did they act like the Joker's henchmen, these Neo-Nazis were covered in racist tattoos all over their fair white skin.

"Speed up, Dane. Fuck these morons!"

Dane pumped the gas but his old beater was no match for the Rambo-Lambo.

"They're gonna ram us, bro!" I yelled. "TURN! QUICK!"

"Your panties juicy already, Codes?" Dane swerved wildly at the last second, avoiding a major collision. "You know I always got one hand on the blunt and one on my cock!"

Should I ask him which hand, then, is on the wheel?

The Rambo-Lambo thundered alongside us.

Time slowed down like it always does when you realize something terrible is about to happen.

I tugged my seat belt on and wished I was driving.

"Welcome back, Dane!" Fisker shouted from the Lambo. Even though he was nearly twenty, he still had a pepperoni pizza face covered in zits. He pulled out an M-16 and aimed it at us. "Dane, you nigger-lover! Now you're home, we're gonna waste your ass!!"

"DOWN!" Dane, instincts still razor-sharp from combat, shoved my head under the dash.

But Dane had nowhere to hide his hulking body as Fisker pulled the trigger—

CLICK.

The chamber was empty.

"Better watch ya back, nigger-lover!!!" Fisker howled, roaring off in the Rambo-Lambo. Fisker had enough hate and fury to rouse Martin Luther King Jr. from his grave.

Dane swerved after them. He popped open the glove box, pulling out his military-issue GLOCK-G21. "They really want fucking war???"

"Fuck you doing?"

Dane reached his hand out the window and fired wildly.

"No. No. NO!!! This ain't fucking Africa!"

All the North Siders in the back of the truck ducked low.

BAM. BAM. BAM.

A bullet ripped through the Rambo-Lambo's windshield.

"Dane, STOP! PLEASE! You're such a fucking moron! You can't do this!"

But he kept shooting.

"The cops are everywhere in Cito! Bet they're coming already."

I looked back. Luckily, I didn't see any police, just grey smoke billowing from the exhaust of Dane's old truck.

The RAMBO LAMBO roared into Riven Rock. One of those Architectural Digest wonderlands where even a tear-down's worth ten mil.

Dane, struggling to keep up, made a screeching wild turn. But the Rambo-Lambo kept pulling further away.

Somehow keeping his balance in the back of the Rambo Lambo, Fisker reached into his pants.

"COME GET SOME, DANE!"

He whipped out his dick.

"THAT'S FUCKING IT!"

Dane aimed carefully this time, making sure he was gonna blast Fisker into the next galaxy when suddenly, A HUMONGOUS TREE-CUTTING TRUCK BACKED out of an enormous drive way.

BEEP-BEEP-BEEP!!!

"LOOK OUT!!" I screamed, grabbing the wheel. I yanked it hard.

Miraculously, we avoided hitting the tree-cutter.

We swerved off the road, smashing into a dry creek bed.

A huge boulder finally put an end to our chase as it crushed the entire front of Dane's truck.

Airbags erupted.

All went black.

CHAPTER TWENTY-THREE

Killer Sushi

5:59 pm

"Cody! Cody!"
I opened my eyes. Looked around.
Dane was okay.
I was okay.
Sirens grew loud in the distance.
I climbed over the smashed door and took off.
I felt kinda bad leaving Dane at the scene of the accident by himself. If the cops connected him to those gunshots, that could spell doom for my best bro. *But let's face it, he'd clearly lost his marbles in the Army. I don't know what the fuck those*

*bastards did to him but he's not the same Dane. No siree, he
went to war a maniac and came back a fucking psychopath.*

I took a bus and skate-boarded my way back to Hope Ranch.

I trudged up the foggy steps toward the polo stables. A frigid
gust of wind blasted my face. Fear and adrenaline ripped
through my stomach. Even though Tiki Torches were lit, illumi-
nating the stone path, the sprawling estate felt deserted.

After stumbling through the mist for several agonizing
minutes, I spotted a dimly-lit stable. A 2Pac remix blasting on a
boom box lured me in. A shiver crawled up my spine when I spotted Eyez and Slim-Dre washing a majestic white horse.

*There was something mad eerie about watching these two
thugs shampooing Mr. Ed.*

Despite the tenderness, I couldn't help but focus all my attention on Slim's massive pistol holstered under his shoulder.

"Glad you finally showed," Eyez washed the suds off his
hands and fired up a vaporizer.

Fear, spreading like a deadly virus from my brain to the rest
of my body, hijacked my legs.

WHOA!

I tripped on a slippery pile of rotting food.

The white horse neighed loudly in the corner.

As struggled to pick myself up, I accidentally put my hand in a
pile of fresh shit.

"GODDAMN!" I screamed.

The White Horse neighed again. Louder. Angier.

Rattled, she raised onto her hind legs.

"Easy, *mi novia.*"

I cowered underneath her massive, majestic body.

Emiliano, polishing his polo mallet, emerged from the shadows. "Bianca likes you! Otherwise she would've crushed you. She
must've smelled all the Benjamin's you have for me."

I stammered, glancing around nervously like a bad actor in an
audition.

Quick!

C'mon, think!

How about I pretend to take an emergency call from The President?

Or, even better, I'll fake a seizure.

Instead, I rifled madly through my pockets. "Oh, fuck... Where is... Wait, hold on, dudes. I left all my cash back at the ride."

Slim-Dre noticed my skateboard. "You calling that piece of plywood a car?!"

The world closed around me in a terrifying moment.

I panicked and dashed for the door but Slim-Dre, surprisingly nimble for his immense body, whipped out a switchblade and blocked me.

I screamed, lifting my skateboard and swinging it wildly. BOOM.

I missed Slim-Dre, hitting Eyez in the shoulder.

He yelled, whipping out a gun and aiming at my temple.

"Please, Emiliano! Just give me one more day! Then you'll have every penny, I promise! What's the fucking difference?"

"Are you slow or something? Did you get extra time on your S.A.T.'s?" Emiliano signaled.

Slim-Dre grabbed me, shoving me onto a table.

"I take that twelve grand," Emiliano pressed the bloody knife against my neck, "put it in a tax-free Roth I.R.A. instead of pissing it away on booze, drugs and pussy like you would. By the time I'm sixty-five, that compound interest is gonna shoot up like a dick on Viagra. So instead of twelve G's we're talking about a quarter-million dollar difference, you fucking jerk-off."

"Haven't I been, up to this point, an awesome employee? Who sold a pound of powder to Jeff Bridges' daughter? Or worked his magic on Oprah's assistant when the big O last rolled through town? You think they'd give you, some Mexican thug, fifteen thousand to make a barrel full of Molly Punch?!"

Emiliano hesitated.

"ISN'T THAT'S WHY YOU TOLD ME TO STAY IN SANTA BARBARA? TO REEL IN THE BIG FISH??" I asked, unable to hold back the tide: "BECAUSE I WAS ALL SET TO GO TO OREGON STATE, REMEMBER?!?"

one year ago:

"**C**ody, we are gonna take this operation so far that you're not gonna have to use Tequila to get women to fuck you." Emiliano squeezed organic limes into a juicer. "When I vacationed with Lance Armstrong's Foundation— Livestrong—Lance was always making *Lanceritas*. Which he said was all about the crushed ice—not the cubes." Emiliano lifted a cocktail shaker over his head and shook it violently. "Growing up, it's all about learning what you like." He poured two delicious drinks, lacing the rims with chili and salt. "Then you grab, make, take, and fake your way till you get it!"

"I'm ready, man! That's why I'm here. To ask your advice."

Emiliano pulled out a massive Ziploc of cocaine.

"So, let's talk about the future, Cody. You gonna go to Oregon State?"

"I received a scholarship. If I maintain a B average they'll float my ride."

"Impressive! That's a very tempting offer. But education—you don't need college for that." Emiliano showed me a faded, mustard-stained napkin full of scribbles and equations he'd framed on his wall. "One night, eons ago, I was at Denny's cramming for a mid-term at Stanford. I must've drunk ten cups of their shitty-ass coffee when I see these Asian dudes across from me. They were the same guys from my class studying for the same stupid test. Heads buried in the textbook as if contained a secret map to the fountain of youth. Suddenly, I realized that we were all rats trapped in a cage. You know what Steve Jobs said?"

"Think different?"

"Exactly, Cody! Society tries to box you in with parameters to live by. Get a nine to five job. Have a family. Mortgage a house. And don't ever bounce into the walls or shake things up. Well, I realized I wanted to shake things up."

"Fuck, yeah. Me too!"

Emiliano grinned, "So I calculated on this napkin how much I would make as a mechanical engineer, my major, versus jumping into the family business."

"Wow. Not even close." I pointed to the X-Y graph. "Think I should skip college, too?"

"Bill Gates, richest man in the Universe, never finished college. But I don't want you to be worried about being the richest. I want you to worry about being the smartest. What's the most valuable thing in the world?"

"Pussy?"

"No. Time. You wanna waste the best four years of your life training to make money? Or you want to start stacking NOW?"

"Emiliano's University? Right here in Paradise City? That's all I'll ever need, huh?"

Emiliano grinned, passing me the small mirror.

There was only one way to seal a deal with the Devil—

By snorting the devil's powder.

present:

6:06 pm

Now, I'm a believer in second chances." Emiliano hovered menacingly over me.

I was tied down onto the chopping block in the stables. The air was putrid and damp. The smell of manure was overwhelming.

I writhed desperately to break free.

"So, yes, I'll grant you that extension. But not a whole day. That's an eternity. I'm giving you till MIDNIGHT!" Emiliano grabbed my skateboard. "So you either adapt and use your brain to scrap together my money—OR DIE!!"

My world froze as Emiliano raised my skateboard high, like a medieval executioner—

"Please! Don't fucking do this!"

"Didn't I promise you all the education you'd ever need? Aren't you glad you took my advice and didn't go to college?"

BOOM—

Emiliano smashed the board down with incredible force.

Right on my nose.
CRACK!
I couldn't stop screaming.

CHAPTER TWENTY-FOUR

No Insurance

6:37 pm

usk. I ripped down the East Beach bike path on my skate. All the tourists were either locked in their rooms sneaking in a quickie before dinner, or here on the sand capturing the glorious sunset with their phones instead of watching with their eyes.

My nose throbbed.

The pain was vicious.

I didn't need a doctor to tell me the obvious—

It was broken.

My phone BEEPED—incoming email from Hopper, my hacker buddy. It read: "CALL ME!!"

The moment of truth had arrived.

Was my dad—or wasn't he—still alive?

Distracted by my screen, I didn't see a hooded bicyclist bearing down on me.

At the LAST SECOND—

I swerved wildly, struggling to maintain my balance on the grass.

CRUNCH!

I slammed into a palm tree, smashing my phone.

Horrified, I picked it up. The screen was shattered.

Frantic, I pushed all the buttons.

Still working!

Relieved, I called Hopper.

But, the phone BEEPED LOUDLY.

The battery was dying.

Only 1%.

"Hello!? Hopper? Can you hear me???"

An ocean of static.

"Cody, brace yourself. I've got... news... won't believe—"

Finally, the line cleared. "Yo, Hopper. Slow down! I can't hear shit. What's the news?"

"Your father. He's—"

Just as he was about to REVEAL THE BIG SECRET—

something I'd desperately wanted to know my whole life—

BOOM—

My phone died.

Fuck!

I tried to light a cigarette but the wind and my trembling hands wouldn't cooperate. Finally, I got the cigarette lit and the smoke felt good in my chest.

Until I started coughing.

Then I spit a disgusting loogie full of blood.

I thought about putting out my cigarette.

You just got your nose broken. *You deserve one.*

"It's illegal to smoke here."

Before I could think of a wise-ass comeback, two uniformed cops grabbed and threw me against the wall.

"You make it way too easy, Cody," Earl said.

Goddamn, I wasn't tripping!

My fucking Probation Officer has been stalking me all day!

"I'm gonna keep frisking you every single day if I have to. Because one time, I'm gonna find all those party favors you carry in your mobile drug store."

"How many times I gotta tell you I ain't dealing?"

Earl stared at my nose. "Then who did this to your face?"

"The Invisible Man sucker-punched me."

"Next time the Invisible Man's gonna chop off your whole, stupid head. And I hope he does! Because you're an embarrassment to everyone of color."

I wanted to hurl back a dirty bomb, but, for once, I shut up.

Earl emptied the contents of my backpack onto the curb.

Thank fucking God I'm all sold out.

Earl grabbed my graffiti black book. Inspected my artwork. "I know it was you who tagged my car. You're the only wanna-be Cito Rat in town. Don't you know the real reason you'll never be a real Cito Brat? I mean, is there even a single non-white dude in Cito?"

I looked away.

"Go ahead. Close your eyes and pretend I'm not here. Because even in sleep, I'm gonna slither so deep into your nightmares, you're gonna have wet dreams about me."

"Fuck do you want, huh? Am I under arrest?"

"I don't ever want to arrest you, Cody. I'd much rather help you fix your life. So why don't you give up your supplier in exchange for getting off probation. Then, just maybe, you can upgrade your wooden Cadillac."

"You don't get it, do you? I like exercising. It's good for *el corazón*. And sure, I'm a wanna-be Cito Rat. But I'll never be your rat? *Comprende*?"

"Full immunity, Cody. Think about a fresh start. Your little crush, Sajda, she would really be proud if you hit reset. You're lucky. She's beautiful. Isn't she worth one smart decision?"

"I'm no snitch."

"Why? What's your boss ever done for you?" He pointed to my mangled nose. "Other than give you an awesome facelift?"

CHAPTER TWENTY-FIVE

S.O.S.

6:49 pm

rgent. I needed to charge my phone. But my face was too bloodied and bruised to use the wireless chargers back at Starbucks. Home was out of the question. So there was only one person I could trust. *Only problem—she's gonna make me play twenty-one questions.*

CHAPTER TWENTY-SIX

Dirty Dancing

6:51 pm

Holding a blood-soaked bandage to my nose and in a tailspin, I stormed through Sak's Fifth Avenue. Wealthy old ladies and their teenage granddaughters threw me horrified looks.

They weren't used to seeing bloody punks in their sanctuary.

Sajda worked behind a counter pushing the latest Lancôme products. She wore an elegant black dress that really made her look grown up.

"MY GOD, CODY!? You can't come in here like this! What happened? You run into Freddy Krueger?"

"Hit this gnarly puddle ripping down Cheski and screeeeeeecchh—the board threw me!" I tried to shrug it off nonchalantly, but I could feel a river of blood bubbling down my nose. "Just gonna wash up real quick."

"Stop lying. Who did this to you?!"

"You crazy? Some asshole threw a Slurpee out the window, I couldn't avoid it. And BAM—I went flying!"

I could tell Saj didn't believe me.

"Codes, I'm taking you to the hospital."

"I don't have insurance."

"That's what credit cards are for, right, Frankenstein Face?"

"Aren't you due for a break? And can I borrow your charger, please? I need to suck some juice."

"You wanna suck on my charger? Again?" Saj asked. "Why'd your stupid phone die so fast?"

She grabbed my arm and took her fifteen minute window of freedom and escorted me down into the bowels of the gigantic store. In the windowless employee washroom, I sat on a sink counter as Sajda changed my bandage. A purple, scabby mess.

So awful she could barely look.

"I've got something I need to come clean about. Truth is, I heard from all the schools I applied to in New York—and unfortu-nately—I got rejected across the board. Every single fucking one."

She shook her head over and over. "Impossible! We spent ages on your app. Re-wrote your entrance essay at least six times!"

"You think they can just do a Google search?" I whispered. "Up pops my name, picture and a warning: 'NOTORIOUS DRUG KINGPIN—DON'T LET HIM DESTROY YOUR COLLEGE.' "

She took a gauze pad and wiped the disgusting pus and blood from my nostrils. Luckily, she found a cool black polo shirt right off a return rack that was my size.

As I changed out of my wet clothes, I shivered uncontrollably. My body was rejecting everything. I felt trapped like I was flying fast to nowhere on a zombie plane.

As Saj went to get me water, I laid down on the floor. So tired, all I wanted do was close my eyes and sleep.

Just for a minute. Maybe two.

"No! You can't sleep!" Sajda rushed back, forcing me to my feet. "You might have a concussion."

She poured me a large glass of water. I started chugging the whole thing.

"Easy, baby," she grabbed the glass. "Sip it."

Just like old times.

Us taking care of each other.

Well, I mean, Saj taking care of me.

"I'm worried for you, Codes. It's not too late. You're more talented than I am for chrissakes! You should be the next Shepard Fairey!"

"You're insane. He's a genius."

"C'mon, how about David Choe, lucky dude made $200 million painting a Facebook mural."

"That's true, all he does is splatter feces, urine, and vomit on the canvas."

"Think about it—is he putting a mirror up to society?"

"Goddamnit, you're right, Saj. If I cruised out with you to NY, we could start that fashion company."

"Exactly. Build a million-dollar brand. An empire. Now, doesn't that sound like an awesome project you'd give your left nut to be a part of?"

"Both nuts."

We laughed, locking eyes—all of a sudden—we were back in eighth grade art class.

She caressed my hand. Her magic fingers sucked all the tension from my body.

"What about Oregon State?"

"I never reapplied."

"But that was going to be your insurance school."

"It was either New York or bust."

"I got a plan—a new plan—you're gonna beg the dean at Oregon State to reinstate that scholarship you turned down like an idiot a year ago. Then, after you do well, you'll transfer to an art school in New York right by me. And we'll be back on track. I promise."

I softened, leaning in closer. "Uh—you know—I've been dreaming about you all day. I want you to be... Us to be... You know—"

"What? Your girl? C'mon, say it. I dare you."

I slid a hand around her waist. Gently kissed her neck. She moaned softly.

Damn, she feels amazing.

"Imagine how cool our baby would be," she whispered, slowly moving her hand down my chest. I lifted up her dress. Bent down slow. Kissed her inner thighs.

"You smoking crack, you old wanker?"

Suddenly—

TWO DUDES BARGED IN, SHATTERING THE MOMENT.

"No way Kobe was ever better than LeBron!" They argued back-and-forth.

"Shit, I'm late." Sajda pulled away. "You're coming to help me tonight, right?"

"You, uh... I really, I wish I could. But if I don't get my paper straight, I might as well put a grenade in my tighty-whiteys."

She fumed, hastily tossing her purse over her shoulder. "Ok, I don't give a fuck if you come or not."

"Hey, who you talking to? Cody? Or some douche bag?"

CHAPTER TWENTY-SEVEN

Real Men Don't Cry

7:08 pm

I cruised outside. My nose felt worse than if I had just snorted a pound of poisoned blow. I popped another few Percocets, but they didn't help. My mind danced around as gracefully as Will Ferrell ice skating on speed.

I hopped on my board and maniacally circled the mall's underground parking lot.

If I don't get some cash quick, I won't just need a nose job, I'll need a heart transplant.

Suddenly, I remembered why I got into this giant mess—

I whipped out my phone and powered it up. The screen was so shattered I could barely hit the buttons to call Hopper.

By some miracle, he picked up right away.

"You trying to kill me with suspense?" I asked.

"Hey, when you know someone is going to hate your gift – do you still give it to them?"

"Wait, what? Are you saying what I think you're saying?"

"I don't know, am I?"

"You never quit with the games, do you?"

Hopper's sudden silence filled me with dread.

"Your father's dead."

"What the fuck you talking about? Are you serious?! I paid ten thousand for this bullshit? I've always known he was dead. Goddamnit!"

Suddenly, I felt very alone.

"Hopper? Hopper? Are you there? Answer!"

Goddamn, another fucking drop call! Again?

I glanced at my stupid phone. Another dropped call!

I wanted to call him back immediately but my hand wouldn't listen. My fingers wouldn't dial. They felt frozen.

Everything—

All of the suffering—

And all of the bullshit Emiliano's put me through—

Has been for nothing!

If only I had found my father—

Then—

Only then—

Would it have been worth it.

God, what a waste!

I'm so pathetic!

10,000 fucking dollars!

Why didn't I give it to Emiliano??

I fought back my tears, but they were already starting to stream down my cheeks.

My watched BEEPED. Another incoming email from Hopper. I clicked on it:

Killer joke, huh?
BTW—
Your dad's still alive.

CHAPTER TWENTY-EIGHT

What are Sisters For?

7:08 pm

y phone flashed with an incoming call. I was surprised to hear a young, terrified voice.
"COOOODDDDYY!!... PLEASE HELP ME!"
I knew instantly who it was. "ASHLEY! WHAT'S HAPPENING? YOU OK?"
"Waaaa–wawaa-ww-wa..."
"Where are you?"

"I, I really n-n-neeeeeeedd—"

"Please, Ash. Pretend I'm standing next to you." All I could hear was her gasping.

Finally, after a long, tortured pause: "I think they're gonna arrest me. You gotta help!"

I could barely believe I was hearing this from my younger sister. "Ashley, what the hell you saying?? You're in jail?"

"N-n-n-n-n-n-nooooo... but I'm-I'm-I'm-I'm-I'm—"

Her petrified voice morphed into an indecipherable, cry.

I'd only heard her like this once before.

When she cut her foot on Butterfly Beach and I had to carry her up a long, windy trail for three miles.

She wailed till her sweet, little throat was raw.

CHAPTER TWENTY-NINE

Diamond in the Sky

7:19 pm

**S**kating furiously through Paseo Nuevo mall, I could tell shit was popping. The latest Tarantino movie had just opened and a long line curved onto State Street. At a small security station, I hopped off my board and gazed through the window.

My heart sank when I saw my sister, Ashley—the little Jail Bird.

Goddamn, what the hell was she doing?

Stealing from this mall?

With a million cameras watching??

Might as well rob the Louvre in Paris!

I marched inside and put my arm around her. She not only looked frightfully pale, but she felt so ashamed she couldn't look me in the eyes.

I approached a security guard with a shaved head. He was monstrously buff, and looked like he could tear a wolf in half with his bare hands.

"How much did she steal?"

"We caught her exiting Sephora with a forty-three dollar mascara kit shoved in her pants."

I glanced back at Ashley. She quickly looked down at the floor. "Do you have to call the police?"

"Not if you can satisfy the situation."

"What's that supposed to mean?"

"I'm not allowed to spell it out for you."

And I didn't need him to.

I whipped out my wallet and threw two c-notes on the table. The guard shook his head, indicating with his thumb that two-hundred dollars wouldn't cut it.

"What kind of bullshit racket you cooking here? What's to stop me from telling your boss? Or reporting you to the authorities?"

"Listen, pal. I thought we could have a more friendly understanding. But if you want to play hardball, that's fine. We can just call the Police. Let them haul your sister to Juvenile Hall."

I wanted to smack this muthafucka in the face.

Instead, I tossed another Benjamin into the pot.

The guard turned to Ashley. "Lucky, your brother is better than a Guardian Angel."

Ashley finally looked up at me—her eyes laced with tears. The guard tore up the incident report from Sephora.

I took Ashley's hand and we maneuvered through the crowded mall. The Solstice excitement was building to a wondrous crescendo.

Ashley was silent as we passed rowdy, overflowing bars. Everyone seemed to be having the time of their life.

I led Ash into Starbucks and ordered blended white-chocolate lattes with double whip. "One thing I know about crime, it makes you really thirsty!"

She inspected the bandage. "What did you do to your nose?"

It was my turn to be silent.

I hailed a cab to take her home.

"I'm glad you called me instead of Mom. She would've kicked you out of the house, too!"

"Maybe I should've! Then we could get a place together! That'd be so fun! I could clean for you and you could help me with my geometry! YES! GOOD PLAN! Fuck Mom and Dad!" She was giddy. The adrenaline and all the crying and all the millions of calories in the Starbucks Frappuccino frying her lid.

"Don't call them that! I, uh, I'd like you to give them a message for me."

"Why? You can always tell them tomorrow, can't you?"

I couldn't explain my situation to my sister.

She was too young.

"Tell Mom, I'm sorry. Tell her... I know she tried her best."

CHAPTER THIRTY

Long Bomb

7:41 pm

Arpan's cellphone rattled with static as he slithered through his enormous grow room. He had over two hundred and fifty budding plants and gave each one of his special ladies a unique name.

I even heard he jizzed in the containers pots to give them extra potency—but unfortunately, this wasn't the time to discuss his secret sauce.

"Hell you wasting my time for, Cody Reese?"

"I've missed you, too, honey bun. You get my text about a friend in need?"

"How come you only call when you got a gun in your mouth, huh? You want me to front you Ketamine and blow? You're getting taxed—three g's."

Talk about a cherry on top! Although it was a ridiculously high price, I had no other option. "You're not gonna stand me up, make me jerk off alone in the mirror? I can really count on you, right?"

"More than you can count on yourself."

I peeked up at the sky and was pleasantly surprised to see a bright, yellow blimp advertising:

DREAM OF ANOTHER LIFE?

The words reverberated through my mind like a shotgun blast.

CHAPTER THIRTY-ONE

Arpan's Last Chance

7:59 pm

I woke up in a fireball of sweat. My brain rattled around but I wasn't trapped in a giant dryer, I was on a bus, bouncing around on a torn-up street. I grabbed a metal bar, jolting in my seat as the bus careened through a roundabout onto Los Carneros Road.

Who the fuck's driving?

Ray Charles?

More important, how the hell did I let myself fall asleep?

Like Sajda said, I probably suffered a mild concussion when Emiliano hammered my nose to shreds. So, if there's a blood clot in my brain, and I fall asleep, I will never wake again.

The bus lurched to a stop. The driver popped open the doors. "Welcome to Hell-a Vista."

I hopped out, jumped on my board and skated through a tsunami of students pushing their way through the streets. Friday night, their objective was simple—get fucked up and do some fucking.

Once I passed the student ghetto, I entered a commercial district where every warehouse was vacant.

Except one.

I kick-flipped to a stop in front of Arpan's medical marijuana grow operation. I marched around the side of the warehouse toward a laboratory in a converted bungalow.

The heavy June fog started to creep in as headlights pierced the night sky. Xenon beams so bright I was temporarily blinded.

An SUV with blacked-out windows swung into the parking lot.

A loud hip-hop remix gave it away.

I froze in terror, watching Emiliano, Eyez, and Slim-Dre exit the vehicle and head towards the laboratory—and me.

My heart pounded.

I struggled to keep calm, hiding around the side of the building, I hugged the walls tight, trying to become one with the shadows.

I wiped a window clean with my shirt and glanced inside.

Arpan, an overly-ambitious Pakistani-American grad student, wearing full HAZMAT suit and face mask, whipped up his patented blend of LSD spiked with MDMA. He worked gracefully with the dangerous chemicals.

SUDDENLY—

The lights flipped off.

A glass shattered.

Arpan screamed for help.

Startled, I crouched extra-low as GUNSHOTS ripped through the night.

A loud POP as the electricity roared back on. All the lights cracked back to life.

Desperate for a better view, I climbed onto a sketchy wooden beam.

What I saw made me sick.

Arpan, sprawled across the floor, clutched a gaping hole above his right knee. He tried in vain to stem the bleeding but it was like plugging a broken dam with bare hands.

Slim-Dre and Eyez dragged Arpan, screaming, and tossed him onto the counter next to the boiling vat of LSD. Emiliano whistled louder than a Superbowl ref. Slim-Dre and Eyez, two obedient robots, left Arpan struggling to breathe and began to rip the laboratory apart.

"I gave you everything. I fucking swear, man!"

"Wrong." Emiliano grabbed Arpan's hand and shoved it in the boiling vat of ACID. Arpan roared in pain. It was a shock to see Arpan so broken. Why would Emiliano wanna hurt Arpan? Doesn't he see the value in a chemist who brews pharmaceutical-grade acid?

Emiliano noticed an award on the desk. Impressed, he held it up, "Arpan Talid. Dean's Award for excellence in physics." He spotted a heavy textbook and leafed through the pages. "String theory. This any good?"

"Yeah."

"Mind if I borrow it?"

Arpan hesitated.

"Don't they teach you in physics never to make false as-sumptions?" Emiliano asked.

I stretched onto my tip-toes, struggling to see the action through the window. As I shifted my weight, the wooden beam CRACKED. I held tight to the window ledge, praying not to make a sound.

Emiliano snapped his fingers in Arpan's face. "The Hadron Collider in Switzerland has already proven string theory true. And now they've confirmed the existence of the mysterious God Particle—"

"Higgs Boson—"

"Six hundred million collisions among three thousand trillion protons every second. Unfathomable, isn't it?"

"We're the same you and me. Science sparks our imagination. Actually, I've been invited to Switzerland on a fellowship. Maybe I—I can pull some strings, call in a few favors and you could visit?"

"Now, wouldn't that special!" Emiliano's face lit up with excitement. "Guys like us, we gotta lotta extra gyri."

"GYRI?" Eyez stopped searching through a drawer. "Fuck's that?"

"Something you eat?" Slim-Dre asked.

"Only if you eat brains." Emiliano peeled on rubber gloves.

"Look, man," Arpan stammered. "I screwed up, I'm sorry. My mom always said I was a fuck up."

I held my breath—if there's one thing I know about Emiliano—he hates neediness.

"One mistake may be forgivable," Emiliano said, "but two—"

"Please! One more—"

"This is not baseball. It's physics. Remember Newton's Third Law?"

"Are you jerking my cock?" Arpan paused. "For every action, there is an equal and opposite reaction."

"Precisely," in a ninja-fast movement, Emiliano grabbed Arpan's head and shoved it in the vat of boiling acid. I shuddered in complete disbelief. A scream rippled through the night, piercing the core of my soul.

C'mon, pussy, do something! You can't just sit here watching him die!

Should I call 9-1-1? Would they even get here in time?

Should I march in there and finally stand up to Emiliano?

Instead of being the hero, I was completely overwhelmed with terror. A horrible cloud of steam hissed from the boiling vat as Arpan's face disintegrated. His body writhed like a fish out of water. His legs and arms flapped until, finally, he stopped.

BOOM—

A loud pop as brain matter splattered onto Emiliano's face. He grinned, "Who wants first crack tasting this batch?"

Emiliano waited for Slim-Dre and Eyez to laugh but they didn't. I shook my head and tried to blast the image of Arpan getting melted like a popsicle on a hot summer's day outta my head.

Am I next??

I reeled in shock, shifting way too much weight onto the center of the fragile beam.

CRACK!

I tumbled down as the ledge ripped from the wall.

A LOUD CRASH as I fell into a thorny cactus. I bit my tongue as the pain rushed through me.

"*Alguien está aquí!*" Emiliano shouted, "*Búsqueda rápida!*"

I spotted Slim-Dre and Eyez exit the lab. Eyez bolted toward the weed warehouse as the hefty Slim-Dre lumbered in my direction. I was in a terrible hiding spot. I knew if I stayed, they'd discover me.

A thunderous ROAR SCREECHED overhead as a FEDEX plane blasted toward LAX. I used the cover of the jet engines to grab my skateboard and hightail it to the beach.

Slim-Dre fired two shots in my direction but the fog was so thick he couldn't see me.

I ran down to the beach, racing along the sand. Behind a cluster of graffiti-covered rocks, I spotted a snorkel and a rusted-out kayak. I hauled the kayak into the water.

Eyez whipped by in a 4WD ATV, zipping along the beach.

Slim-Dre setup a high-powered sniper rifle on the cliff line.

Now or never!

I whipped out a newspaper and lighter fluid from my back-pack. I threw everything including my skateboard into the kayak. I sparked my Zippo.

The backpack caught fire.

I sprayed more lighter fluid—
WHOOSH!

I pushed the blazing kayak out to sea.

The fire flared so bright it lit up the night.

Eyez and Slim-Dre took the bait, racing toward the kayak.

By the time they figured out they'd been duped, I'd used the snorkel to swim, undetected, all the way to UCSB, where I rode the current into the campus lagoon.

CHAPTER THIRTY-TWO

Chasing the Dream

10:26 pm

glanced at my Apple Watch, scrolling through the file I received from Sabu69. I still had trouble wrapping my head around it. *My father's still alive! And is he really living only thirty miles away in Oxnard?*

I stared at an old DMV photo of him—the only one Sabu could find—over fifteen years old.

Dude's whiter than the moon.
Could this surfer burnout really be my dad?
Looks like a washed-up Tom Hanks after years alone on a deserted island with only his volleyball, Wilson.
Something's gotta be wrong.
Next to the photo was a phone number.
I took a deep breath and dialed.
It rang.
And rang.
And rang.
Strangely, there was no voicemail.
I was about to hang up when a man answered.
"Herlo? Heeerlo?" The hoarse voice was thicker than a half-blended smoothie. "Anybody home? Peek-a-boo!"
I couldn't believe it really was him. After all these years wondering and dreaming and hoping.
Here he is—
Dear Old Dad!
I was so overwhelmed, my lips formulated words but nothing came out.
"Hello? Answer, you shit! Whoever this is, I can hear you breathing. It better not be you punk ass kids again! If it is, I'll come find you and kill you."
The man hung up.
I stared at the receiver, still in shock.
Was that really him?
He sounded awfully mean. Goddamnit, I already got enough stress going on.
Do I really need to put myself through this?
My therapist told me I have obvious abandonment issues.
Do I really need to rock this boat? What if I finally meet him and he rejects me again?
Could I handle that?
Suddenly, the screen flashed with a frantic text from Sajda:

WHERE R U?! I NEED YR HELP!! NOW!!

Sure, I can handle fucking up with Emiliano.
But Sajda?
Can I leave her hanging too?

CHAPTER THIRTY-THREE

Plastic Love

9:08 pm

I entered a plush downtown photo studio. Cutting-edge 4K monitors lined the walls. A photographer with Gandalf grey hair and a perfect surfer-tan barked orders at his gaffers to pump up the overhead lighting. "Get that HMI with 2K ballast on standby, we're gonna want a nice, hard, Hollywood backlight."

Three models, a pale Russian, a freckly red-haired beauty, and an Israeli transfer-student, received 'last looks' by makeup and hair stylists. A seamstress helped Saj make last minute adjustments to her outfits. A Photoshop technician loaded test images onto thunderbolt drives as his iMac rendered effects.

Not only was I blown away by the army Saj had assembled, I also patted myself on the back for not being a selfish asshole—*thank God I didn't try to force her to cancel this shoot and fork over every penny she had.*

"Alright, Mr. No Show makes an appearance," Sajda said.

I slapped her a big high-five. "How much you spend on this extravaganza?"

"Let's just say, I totally understand now whenever someone says, 'the budget spiraled out of control.' "

"Two thousand?"

She pointed at all her minions helping make the shoot awesome. "Higher."

"Three thousand???"

"Look how incredibly talented my photographer is—and his three assistants—and color correction specialist!"

"Thirty-five hundred?"

She nodded. I was flabbergasted, struggling not to think about if she'd given me all that dough. Would that have been enough to appease Emiliano?

"Of all the days I need your help, you have to get your face busted

You're all I got, Codesta."

That's what I loved about Sajda.

Refusal wasn't an option.

"Lucky I'm such a good nurse," she gently peeled off the bandage. "It's swollen pretty bad but at least it doesn't look like I'm dragging in the homeless."

"Still think I'm sexy?" I made a silly pose in the mirror. "Cause I know I'd fuck me."

She handed me a grey suit she'd sewn and designed. It was a little too small but I squeezed in. I grabbed a turban and put it over my head. Then I popped on my sunglasses.

"Love the look, Codes!" One of the models yelled across the studio. "More mysterious than Carlos the Jackal."

I smiled at my reflection in the mirror. "I'm a James Bond terrorist."

"Ready?" the photographer shouted. His lighting team blasted the room with artificial smoke and cranked up a ginormous fan. I bounced onto the catwalk and busted some dance moves. Everyone cracked up, including the photographer. I could tell he was one cool dude and probably slayed a few dragons during his youth.

"Bold choice, Sajda." The photographer fired off a sequence with his 85mm prime. "I love the bruised nose! Looks like he just manhandled a few wise guys from the *French Connection.*"

"Hear that, Cody? You saved my shoot." Sajda pinched me on the ass.

The other models hovered around me. After a barrage of photos and poses, Sajda called for a timeout. "Take three. I'm gonna grab a couple more hijabs I got buried in my trunk."

Right as Saj exited, a voluptuous model with highlighter-pink hair signaled me. Finger to the nose, Roxy wanted to know if I was holding the powwow.

I nodded. She handed me a few bills, asking for two. I marched into the bathroom to check my stash. I barely had enough for half a gram. But goddamn. I felt so desperate. With my busted nose and pain killers clouding my judgment

It was time—

TO BREAK MY CODE!

In a cabinet under the sink, I found some dusty makeup supplies. I mixed talcum powder with the coke, stretching it all the way to Timbuktu. I couldn't help but feel crazy guilty as I gave it to Roxy. But, most important—

I dropped the two baggies in her hand—and didn't let go.

Not till—

"I PROMISE I WON'T."

"Saj is paying for everything outta pocket. If she even suspects, she will kill me."

"I never get high working. Ever."

CHAPTER THIRTY-FOUR

Oath-Breaker

9:29 pm

"I was so worried you were gonna flake, Codes!" Sadja massaged my back gently. "But here we are, with front-row seats, watching this incredible artist perform."

"You're the real artist, my dear." The photographer smiled warmly. "All I do is flip on a light or two and press the trigger."

"When you submit your portfolio to the Tim Gunn fellowship," I whispered in Saj's ear, "not only will he let you in the class. I bet he'll hire you, too!"

"And I can always pull the Muslim card if he hesitates."

"That's my Saj," I slapped her another high-five. "Always willing to bend the rules."

The photographer gave me a friendly pat-on-the-back as he switched lenses. "Your boyfriend brought a great chemistry to the set."

"Yeah," Sajda winked. "Boyfriend."

First time anyone's ever called me 'boyfriend.'

And you know what—

It sounded AWESOME.

"WHOA!!! WHAT HAPPENED?!" The photographer screamed across the room. "YOU OK?!??"

Everyone raced over to check out the commotion. Roxy and Jenny, another model, frantically tried to plug their bleeding noses with paper towels.

The photographer couldn't believe it. "Did you step on a rake?!"

Fucking Roxy broke her damn promise!

I wanted to scream. Instead, I snuck into the bathroom and checked out the talcum powder I mixed with the blow. After smelling it a couple times, I came to a horrifying realization.

It definitely wasn't talcum powder. So what the fuck was it?

And God forbid, what if these two chicks die?

Goddamn dealers have been cutting their powders, potions, and elixirs for millennia—going back to the first Witch Doctor cooking up Bitches Brew. *This isn't even my first rodeo and here I am biting the donkey on the dick.*

As I exited the bathroom, Saj grabbed me. "You monster! What did you give those two girls?"

Roxy, scared, looked to me for guidance. I wanted to smack her with my belt.

What'd you do, fucking twat? Pull a Kate Moss?

Snort the whole fucking bag?

I remained silent as Roxy squirmed in the hot seat. She had ten napkins shoved up her nostrils and still that wouldn't stem the blood flow. "It's really super dry today... and um, I've got terrible, awful allergies."

"CALL A FUCKING AMBULANCE!" The photographer barked. "It's Night of the Living Dead, Sajda. We're done."

Saj looked to me for answers. I tried to shrug it off. "Was just a little nose candy. Nothing craze."

"Nothing craze? You think it's OK to just toss my three thousand, five hundred dollars out the window? And blow the biggest chance I've ever had?"

I reached out to her.

She glared at my hand like I was offering her a delicious, AIDS burrito. "I want you out—forever."

"You don't mean that! Listen, Saj, wait—"

She slapped me.

Not soft like a girl.

More like a freight train.

BAM—

The third hit was her HAIL MARY.

She smacked my broken nose. I screamed in agony as a geyser of blood erupted from my face.

Maybe it was just my luck, but this time, something told me she wouldn't be making me another tender bandage.

CHAPTER THIRTY-FIVE

Rich as Shit

9:56 pm

Even though I still owed Emiliano a bucket of money, I had to see with my own eyes if my father was what everyone said: *A big fucking loser.* I was hoping—I was determined to prove them wrong.

As I sat in the back of a rundown IHOP that had seen better days, I couldn't let of go of the dream that maybe—just maybe—my real dad's a millionaire.

I waited for my father, keeping my eyes glued to the door. Only problem, I didn't know what the fuck the dude looked like so I prayed he wore a name tag. All I knew was the guy sounded like he woke up every day to the breakfast of champions: Marlboro Reds and whiskey straight.

My heart pumped faster as a handsome, older gentleman entered wearing a Stetson hat. The man walked right up to me, locked eyes, and then kept going. He parked in a booth and was joined by a slender woman. Although she wasn't exactly a looker, she had long legs that begged for investigation. I spotted her blood-red underwear beneath her skirt. "Excuse me," I said to them, wondering if she was going to be my stepmom, "are you supposed to meet someone here?"

They shook their heads. Disappointed, I noticed a fat Sheriff enter the restaurant. Is that him? Could my dad enforce the law? Would that be cool?

The Sheriff threw a $20 bill on the counter, grabbed his takeout and left.

An old surfer staggered out of the bathroom. He wore plaid shorts and what looked like a pizza and cum-stained tank top. Not only did he have scraggily hair that hadn't been washed in weeks, the dude looked like he slept under a pier with slimy crabs. He was walking algae personified.

"Eww," I groaned in disgust. The guy caught me looking. I gazed at my phone, pretending to browse Instagram.

"Cody Reese???"

I turned around and there was the old surfer, towering over me. Don't let this be him. Don't let this be him.

I shook my head. "You looking for a Cody? Cody who?"

"Yeah, about your age. We were to meet in the back."

"Wish I could help you."

"Whatever," the old-timer wandered around the joint like a hungry dog sniffing for his bowl. I couldn't take my eyes off the oil spill of a man.

The old dude put a quarter in a gumball machine. The coin got stuck. He pounded the machine furiously—still no candy popped out. A Korean waitress who barely spoke English, tried to calm him down. "It ate my fucking money!" The old man kicked the machine.

I rushed over. "He's, uh—he's with me!"

The man, surprised, threw me a confused look. But I ushered the old dude back to my booth before he could embarrass me any further.

"So you are Cody, huh? Why'd you lie?"

"It's weird seeing you, I guess."

"Well, I don't wanna be here if you don't want me to."

"No, I do. I mean, stay. Please. I've been picturing this day for an eternity—"

"Here's Johnny! Ready for my close-up!" His father flashed what would've been a million dollar grin except he was missing two teeth and the ones he had were stained vomit-yellow.

"Your name's Johnny?" I asked, surprised.

"No, I'm Rich."

As we shook hands, I was surprised by my father's iron grip. "Where the fuck ya been all these years?" I blurted out, desperate for an answer to the big question.

A long silence. Rich seemed only half-here. His body was here, but his spirit, his soul, if he had one, was elsewhere.

Probably at Legoland.

The Korean waitress interrupted our deep connection. "Ready?"

"Two beers. Coronas." He winked at the waitress. "And we can just keep our sweet little secret between us, right honey?"

"Yes, of course, sir," she said, awkwardly. "But I need to see your son's I.D. first."

"What kinda of crooked joint you running here?" he erupted. "Want me to burn this place down? Cause I will."

"My father's only joking," I said to the scared waitress, handing her an ID card. She frowned, checking the phony dates. "Ok, two Coronas."

Rich stuck his tongue out as she left. "What a bitch, huh?"

"Don't sweat her, that's why I got my fake I.D., right?"

"You good-looking devil! But wait, you're twenty-one, aren't you?"

"Sssssssh," I whispered.

"Stop lying. You're already a man. Look at you."

I don't know what was worse. The fact my dad didn't know my age. Or that he had a bad receding hairline. Fuck, is that gonna happen to me, too?

We drank our beers in silence. Although my mind burned with questions, I felt paralyzed as if my vocal cords weren't on the same team with my brain.

Suddenly, an angry text message from EMILIANO:

ALMOST MIDNIGHT, LITTLE SLUT,

READY TO SLAP THE CASH IN MY PALM?

I tried to ignore the threat, but it was like shaking off a light-ning-bolt from Zeus. Finally, the bill arrived.

"My treat." Rich dropped a ten on top of the check and pulled out his Marlboros. "Wanna ciggie?"

He ambled out the door toward the parking lot.

I gathered my belongings and glanced at the bill. *Even though my dad offered to treat, he was still short.*

I sighed, dropping another $10 on the table.

Outside, a soft rain drizzled down. "Don't you love the rain? Everything smells so fresh—gets me off!" Rich tasted the raindrops on his tongue like he was a young boy. "Still can't get over how good-looking you are. I tell you I used to model?"

As Poster Boy for a rehab clinic?

I wanted to ask. But then I remembered, just an hour ago, my own modeling disaster.

"Don't be fooled by this beer belly. I used to get paid to travel the globe! And yes, of course, I drove the girlies crazy."

"What happened?"

"I met your mom."

"And then?"

"See all these lines on my face? Where you think those came from?"

"My real mother was tough?"

"Just the opposite! She was something else. Wow! But our stars never lined up. I'm a Scorpio and she was a Leo."

"How can you blame the fucking stars? They're billions of light-years away."

"*Duh.* Their energy influences ours. Where do you think us humans get all our power?"

Power?

I stared at the hippy-looking necklace around Rich's neck with a large crystal attached. "From our opposable thumbs?"

"The sun. Without its constant nuclear explosions, we wouldn't be here."

"Still, what does that got to do with you and my mother?"

"Although I'm lucky at getting laid, I can't keep a woman. Even with super glue."

I almost felt sorry for the old bastard.

C'mon, don't be a wimp. Ask the question you've been WAITING YOUR WHOLE LIFE TO ASK.

"Is that why you abandoned me after she died?"

"Hey, your mom abandoned us. She took the easy way out! Left both of us alone."

What's he talking about, 'easy way out?' She died in a car accident. But I didn't wanna start World War 3.

"Please, can you help me out? Didn't you at least keep one photo?"

Rich didn't answer.

"Please, I'm trying to picture her! Just tell me something! Anything. Please!"

A long pause.

"One day your mother said she was part American Indian. Another day she would say she was part Tahitian. It was always something different but I didn't care. She was beautiful and I just loved to..."

"You NEVER ONCE asked where she was from?"

"Mystery always makes sex better, don't you agree?"

The thought of this old, disheveled buzzard having sex made me want to puke.

A fiery meteor burned across the night sky, basking us momentarily in the golden blaze. "Think your mother's riding that comet, right now?" Rich asked. "Blasting across the galaxy on bitchin' adventures?"

I frowned.

Somehow the thought of my mother burning to cosmic dust in the atmosphere didn't sound that epic.

Then, something truly weird happened—

Rich put his arm awkwardly on my shoulder. And, even though the bastard smelled like he'd been chasing El Chapo down Mexican sewers gushing with rivers of diarrhea—

Rich's hand felt oddly comforting.

Like his hand had been on my shoulder for eternity. Then, Rich took the ultimate final step toward actually becoming my real father. Whether truth or fiction, he saw my soul was wounded. And he told me magic words to soothe my anxiety.

"Hours after you were born, your mother was glowing, unable to stop squeezing and smiling at you. So completely drunk with glee. Her usual tough shell melted away. I wanted to kiss her but she said that instead, we should rub our noses together. "That's how my ancestors, the Alaskan Eskimos, kept their loved ones warm while they crossed the Bering Strait."

ACROSS THE BERING STRAIT?!

I took comfort in this thought. It gave me a surge of strength. Of hope. Suddenly, my busted nose didn't hurt so much anymore.

But more important, all of a sudden—

Emiliano didn't seem like that much a badass anymore!

Rich inspected my tan lines caused by immeasurable hours in a wetsuit. "I'm proud you surf, son. That's my only true love. Especially, now that my dick stopped working."

I wanted to ask him about his broken dick but felt like it could wait. "Let's go hit the waves sometime."

"Think my saggy ass can keep up?"

"Only one way to find out."

We jammed back to his van to smoke a doobie. He had an old Volkswagen that had seen a million parties. I was shocked to learn that he camped in the back of this love wagon at Burning Man, Coachella, BPM and every epic music fest from here to Patagonia.

"Why waste precious dough on a hotel, right?" Rich opened a cooler. He pulled out two cold-ones, tossing me a bottle. I took a big drink, grabbing an acoustic guitar from the front seat. I banged out a few power chords. Rich banged on a conga drum and sang, "Shell shock, battle fatigue, absolute insanity—"

I joined in. "Flashback, panic attacks, death's riding—gunning for me!"

"You are my son! You bastard!!" A big high-five.

"We sound bitchin', Dad."

"Better than bitchin'! You know, I'm really glad you called."

We looked at each other for a long, heartfelt moment.

I could barely whisper. "Me, too."

Rich took off his turquoise necklace. "Your mother would have liked you to have it."

"Wow!" I inspected the sparkling gemstone. "This is serious bling! Must be worth a fortune!"

"She gave me this when we met. Back in Taos, New Mexico, when it was wasn't overflowing with yuppies."

"Is it worth nine thousand?"

Rich laughed. "Not all value can be written on a price tag. Besides, I'm not giving it to you to sell."

"So it's worthless?"

"It's imitation silver."

I frowned. "Man, Dad, that's uh... I, uh, hate to ask you this but I need to. I'm in serious fucking trouble."

Rich blew a kiss to the stars twinkling light years away. "Fate brought us back together, son. You found me at a critical juncture in your life."

He put his arm around me.

First time my real dad ever put his arm around me!

"Did you see that comet? Ha! It's a message. The Universal Spirit reunited us so I can guide you."

"Uh, that's awesome. Really. But I'm in way fucking deep. I don't think I can wiggle out of this one. And I'm not sure if the constellations or the Milky Way galaxy can help. What I wanna ask—What I hate to ask you—I need money, Dad. Right away."

"Money, what's that? The devil's drug."

"Please, c'mon, Dad. I've never ever asked you for anything my whole life."

"I know what will fix your problems. You leave everything to me, baby boy."

Rich packed a glass pipe with an enormous bowl. "Besides, this is way better than nine grand. It will guide you back to the light."

"What'd you sprinkle on top? Hash?"

"Hash isn't going to solve your problems. This is Angel Dust."

"PCP?!?" I coughed out a huge cloud of smoke. "How the fuck's that gonna help?"

CHAPTER THIRTY-SIX

Hand for a Hand

10:17 pm

My dad was an even bigger disappointment than I could have ever imagined. Not only did he have just one foot in reality, but the other foot was somewhere in the Milky Way.

After I turned down his PCP, Rich opened up, revealing a desperate existence. Living out of his van. In and out of jail. Years lost in a fog in a mental hospital.

A complete whack-job.

Still, goddamnit!

He was my father!

And although he may have abandoned me all those years ago, I'm gonna be different.

I'm gonna help the poor bastard.

Otherwise I'm gonna end up just like him—

A fucking loser.

I decided to do what I always do when the going gets tough—

I hit the beach, hurrying across the sand.

I climbed a wall.   Hopped over a small fence.

Homeless, and my life in my backpack, I was at a dead end. So I did what I always do when the going gets tough, I hit the beach. I hurried across the sand. Climbed a wall. Hopped over a small fence.

Suddenly, I was at the Coral Casino.

Montecito's playground for the ultra-rich. An Olympic size pool. Cabanas. Piano player. The kinda place where people looked at you funny if you weren't worth at least twenty mil.

I wrapped a gold towel around my board shorts and tried to look as if I belonged. I spotted a sexy MILF that half the guys in Santa Barbara have hooked up with. She waved. She was wearing a revealing bathing suit from Dolce & Gabbana.

"Don't cumsies in your shorts," a voice said.

I noticed Theep in the hot tub. He was Russian. Mid-fifties in Speedos. Exuded confidence and power. I jumped into the hot tub. I ducked my head in the water and stayed under for a few seconds.

As I resurfaced, I found Theep staring at me. "Where are your wild friends?"

"It's just me. Listen, I hate to ask you this..." I hesitated. "But I need a loan, man. Or I'm gonna get hurt."

"You mean, there's gonna be more damage to your beautiful face? We can't let that happen. You're my Ulysses. How much you need?"

I swallowed. "Nine g's. Can you front me? I'll pay you back soon. With interest. I promise."

Theep smiled, sliding closer. "Before we talk numbers, how about we pop some champagne and enjoy the sunset? I'm sure we can work out an arrangement."

He led me back to his immaculate cabana stocked with booze. Theep poured a crystal bottle of Patron into two glasses loaded with ice. "Cheers, baby."

I tried not to shudder every time he called me his 'baby.' *Block it out, man. It'll be over in a few seconds and you'll have the money. Honestly, is it too late in the day to put my kidney up for sale on eBay?*

Theep, excited, closed the linen curtains. "Nine thousand is a small price for a prince like you."

I laughed awkwardly. *Man, it's claustrophobic in here. Has the room gotten smaller?*

"Mind if I get the cash up front?"

"So you can run away and we don't get to play?" Theep giggled. "Where's the fun in that?"

"C'mon, dude."

"Relax, Cody." Theep poured me another drink. "I just want us to hang out."

He put his hand on my ass. I shifted away. "Don't be nervous. I'm gentle." Theep sat on the bed. "Take off your shirt."

Fuck that.

Theep looked at me expectantly. I reluctantly took off my shirt.

"Ooohhh!" Theep squealed like a thirteen-year-old at a Justin Bieber concert. "Come sit on the bed with me."

I reluctantly sat down. Theep ran his hand across my muscles. I winced. Closed my eyes. Theep leaned over me. "Pretend I'm Miley Cyrus."

I'd have an easier time pretending you were a cup of coffee.

"Oh, my. You got a boo-boo. Let me make it better for you." Theep was about to kiss my bandage.

"Fuck this shit." I grabbed my shirt and bolted to the door.

"Hey, I thought you liked being different?"

CHAPTER THIRTY-SEVEN

Border Jumper

10:43 pm

hurried into the train station and bought a ticket for the next train out of town. I paced endlessly. I blew a good-bye kiss to the gargantuan Morton Bay Fig Tree, the soul of Santa Barbara, and asked a baggage handler. "How far does this train go?"

"Seattle."

Not far enough.

But I can hike across the border and skate right into Vancou-ver.

A whistle blew and the engine roared to life.

I marched toward the train as Dane, across the street, exited Channel Islands Surf Shop carrying two surfboards. He tossed them into his pickup.

I ducked low. *C'mon, muthafucka, be invisible.*

He waved and shouted my name, hurrying over to stop me. He erupted in fury when he saw my busted nose. "Didn't I tell you that piece of shit would tear your scrawny ass up?"

"Take it easy, will you?"

"Why don't you want my fucking help? Haven't I known you since before you first spanked your dong?"

I turned to board the train but Dane ripped my bag from my hand. "Where you think you're going?"

"I can't stay here."

"Think the number one army in the world, the USofA, earned that position by running away? C'mon, let's go somewhere we can really think."

CHAPTER THIRTY-EIGHT

Two Musketeers

10:53 pm

 few hundred yards down the train tracks, behind a noisy stinky recycling center, I whipped out a can of blood-red spray paint, twisted on a fat cap and tagged the train tracks behind the 101 freeway:

"Now, that I've found my rock-star dad, you're the only Fatherless Bastard left," I said.

Dane pulled out his Glock-21 and tossed a whiskey bottle into the sky. "There's one last option we haven't discussed yet, mi amigo."

BOOM—

Dane shot the bottle mid-flight like a cocky gunslinger. "Unless, you'd rather tuck your tail between your pussy and run?"

Feeling truly out of hope, I picked up a rock and chucked it at a telephone pole.

Missed.

I angrily threw another and, of course, missed again.

"I just got back from fighting Boko Haram. Where's my ticker-tape parade? And Saj, I've called her a million times. She won't even answer a text."

I avoided his gaze.

"You and her get into a fight?"

I felt my cheeks turn red.

"Don't tell me. No, you didn't. She's like our sister, bro. You don't bone your sister. That's disgusting."

I grabbed Dane's beer and took a long pull. "She's pregnant."

"Wow! Seriously? That's a beautiful thing."

"You loco? Think I wanna have a fucking baby?"

"Well, you should've thought about that before you dumped a fat load of jizz in her."

The words stung.

"What's crazy, for real, is that even if you and Saj were the worst parents ever, you'd still be better than one thousand percent of the fucked-up madness I witnessed in Africa."

"Life was cheap there?"

"Worthless! You think Emiliano's shoving your feet in the fire? Imagine a monster far worse than him on every street corner. Ready to rape, steal, or kill. Who'd cut out a newborn's heart and feast on it before it stops beating!"

"Why??"

"They believe consuming an innocent heart before battle makes 'em invincible."

I patted my oldest friend on the back. I loved Dane because he was like a comic book superhero, dedicated to wiping bad guys off the face of the planet.

"I..." Dane whispered, "killed a heavy hitter on the CIA payroll."

"A CIA agent?"

"Mobotu. A prized informant. But also a Boko Haram monster responsible for murdering thousands. And those he didn't kill directly, he starved. I witnessed that muthafucka slaughter Nigerians begging for food. Sliced 'em down with a machine gun."

"Jesus Christ, Dane, you had to make the war personal, didn't you?"

"Mobotu was committing a war crime. Any soldier with a shred of humanity would've..." Dane paused, reliving the trauma. "I grabbed my rifle. Pulled the trigger. And BOOM. Blasted his ass away."

"So that's why you said there's no room in the Army for The Lone Ranger, huh? For killing *this strategic asset*? Now they wanna shit-can you?"

"In six weeks I'm gonna be court-martialed."

I gazed at Dane, finally understanding his anger. Now I could see why he longed to return to his unit—now that he started making the world a brighter place—it was addictive—he couldn't stop.

A coastal train roared past. In the caboose, a group of college boys and girls flashed their bare asses. Everyone hollered in excitement. One of the sorority girls flung a beer at Dane. He deftly whipped out his gun and shot it mid-air.

"Well, sweet Caroline, will you look at that. I know exactly what we need to do! I can't believe I didn't think of this before because it combines all our best skills.... Ok, ready? Drum roll, please." Dane paused, maximizing the effect. "We're gonna throw a party!"

I sighed. "How come when the going gets rough, your solution is always to rock-out with your cock out??"

"A rager to end all ragers—and we'll charge every cat in town ten bucks."

"Ten Bucks? We'd need nine hundred people to show. Even if we could miraculously make that happen, you really think your mom's gonna give us the green light to rage while she's upstairs dying of cancer?"

Dane smiled. "Who said anything about asking her?"

CHAPTER THIRTY-NINE

Burning Down the House

11:27 pm

All the neighbors for miles could hear the epic party. Forget the postcard-perfect beaches or hills of the Riviera. No doubt, the place to be that night was Dane's mansion. A huge crowd, including a lotta hot chicks in fuck-me-outfits, surrounded Dane, who took full advantage of the event to test out some new jams he'd been working on in his music studio. He had an electronic punk sound and enough smoke machines, lasers and strobe lights to turn his stage, a skateboard half-pipe, into a full-blown rave.

"Minimalism is for pussies!" he screamed, closing his eyes and channeling his hero, Jimi Hendrix. Dane ripped into his 12-string guitar.

But then he hit a few wrong notes. Chuckles and mocking laughter pierced the night. Loud boos filled the air.

Dane kept playing, more and more ferociously, ripping into a roaring solo.

Behind him, a fat black dude with an afro and a smile so big it looked like it was drawn on with a crayon, kept tempo on a steel drum set. A skinny goth bassist, who looked like he survived on a strict diet of heroin and Lucky Charms, struggled to keep up with Dane's intensity.

Standing next to several kegs and a makeshift bar, I held an enormous Costco-size bag of red plastic cups while people waited in line to pass me their cash. "Anything for a good cause." A kid handed me crumpled one-dollar bills. "This really a non-profit fundraiser?"

I grinned. "This party is gonna save lives."

After Dane finished his brief set, we counted up all the cash I'd collected. "In twenty minutes we've already raked in one thousand, seven hundred dollars, but we've only got a half-hour till midnight. Well, fuck, let's pray."

"Since when is prayer a plan?" Dane stepped into the crowd.

I looked up as the Rambo-Lambo, trailed by two F-350 pickups with insanely loud country music blaring, roared to a stop at the back of the house. Big swastikas on the bumpers. A horde of gnarly white dudes stepped out.

THE NORTH SIDERS.

I hurried to warn Dane they were here when all the lights and music cut out.

"Hey, I can't see!" "Fuck's going on?"

Girls screamed their friends' names to find each other. A cacophony of "Lexi?" "Sarah?" "Hannah?" "Where are you?"

A tornado of bumping bodies.

I finally found Dane. "Fucking North Siders must've cut the fuse. We gotta reset the breaker before everyone leaves!"

CHAPTER FORTY

Sinking in Quicksand

11:35 pm

ane and I, flashlights in hand, frantically searched the garage for the fuse box. We found Fisker, the same North Side asshole from earlier. You remember the Douche in the Rambo Lambo who pointed an M-16 at Dane?

I rushed toward Fisker, but Dane pulled me back. "Easy, fool, you're the brains. I'm the Terminator!"

Dane charged Fisker. But Dane was too drunk and sloppy. Fisker deftly dodged to the side and grabbed his arm, twisting in fury.

SNAP!

Dane roared in pain.

I rushed to help but Dane was so wasted, he kicked me in the chest with a wild roundhouse kick.

I reeled back, crashing into a metal shelf. Heavy boxes stuffed with old Polaroids crashed onto my head.

Fisker grabbed Dane's long hair and smashed him into the wall. Blood splattered across Fisker's face as he pulled out a pistol.

"Of course, you'd bring a gun to a fist fight!" Dane snarled.

Fisker clicked off the safety. Dane took his final breath.

BOOM.

I cracked my skateboard on the back of Fisker's head.

"Where were you? Putting on your lipstick?"

We hurried back outside to find that the North Siders had destroyed, smashed, eaten and pissed on everything in their path. They had filled their trucks with all our kegs and liquor bottles.

Dane and I sprinted after them. But they gunned their trucks out of the drive. Country music roared as the North Siders disappeared down Olive Mill road and into the heart of Montecito.

CHAPTER FORTY-ONE

Beer Funnel

11:39 PM

"What am I gonna give Emiliano now?! All I got out of this fucked-up party is seventeen-hundred." I surveyed the wreckage left by the North Siders. "Everything was going so smooth, too! Motherfucker! Fuck. Fuck. Fucking shit!"

A group of high-schoolers I recognized from the tennis team approached. "What are we supposed to drink now? You owe us a REFUND!"

"I owe you? How the fuck do I know it wasn't you who tipped off the North Side?"

"Because I'm Mexican, asshole."

"Oh, yeah, Pancho Villa? You wanna start some shit?" Furious, I stepped in the dude's grill. Dane pulled me back. "Calm down, ese."

"I don't even give a shit anymore," I said. "Honestly, we should just rip up the 192 to the peak of Gibraltar mountain! Drop some gnarly acid. Then jump off the cliff."

I shadowed Dane through the mansion as he proceeded to lock down anything that might get stolen or broken. He padlocked the medicine cupboard.

"These pills are for us only, right Codes?" Dane popped a Xanax.

From the next room, we heard a strange sound. Loud, horrible. Like a diesel train engine struggling to climb a steep mountain.

"Whoa! Is that snoring? Sounds like a Rhino herd."

"Mom's got sleep apnea, too."

"Jesus, is there actually a fatal disease she doesn't possess?"

I followed Dane over to his mom.

"I'm glad you're still snoring, mom. It means you're not—"

A booming fart erupted from Dane's mom. But, at least that was announced.

Her second was a silent but deadly attack that left both of us gasping.

The third was another booming fart that vibrated loudly.

"Save it for the show, ma!"

She looked bony, fragile, and extremely weak. But, then, like a hibernating Komodo Dragon, a deep thunder awoke her spirit.

"Don't forget me," she said. "OK?"

"How could I? You taught me everything about being independent and taking care of myself. How to date. You always warned me about the skanks, remember?"

"It takes one to know one." She giggled.

Dane was getting emotional, struggling to speak. "I'll never look back and say, oh, my mother was a... I'll always look back and think, 'wow, she gave me a lotta love.' Really, Ma. I do..." Instead of finishing the sentence, he draped a warm blanket over her shivering body. "I'll keep everyone out. No one will disturb you."

"I just hope my pain stays this way until I close my eyes in the coffin."

CHAPTER FORTY-TWO

Sudden Death

11:59 pm

I moved nervously through the party. Even though the booze was gone, the joint was rocking past the point of insanity.

Unfortunately—Emiliano, surrounded by Eyez, Slim-Dre and a few other gnarly-motherfuckers, strutted through the gates. His crew didn't need to push their way through the crowd. Everyone was so intimidated by them they stepped aside, parting like the Red Sea.

Dane put an arm on my shoulder. "What you gonna do?"

"I don't fucking know!" I threw up my hands. "Lemme think, bro, lemme think."

"Maybe you can work out some kinda weekly payment plan?"

"Does Emiliano look like a fucking loan counselor?"

I spotted a squad of cheerleaders, laughing, drinking, and looking incredibly sexy in short rah-rah outfits. Right in the center was the lovely Tinker Bell.

Remember the knockout I told you about at City College?

She winked at me.

Dane followed my gaze to the cheerleaders. "Thinking with your dick, again?"

"Actually, for the first time in my life, I'm staring at babes and not thinking about sex. I'm thinking about chemistry, Dane. You remember that pill you put aside for your mother? That one that makes skin blue?"

"It's in my wallet, why?"

"Get a hold of Butt-Crack Benito. Tell him to get the fuck over here."

CHAPTER FORTY-THREE

Last Breath

12:03 am

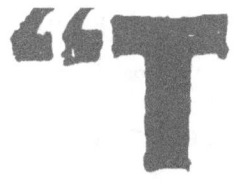hanks for not making me come chase you."
"Maybe I'm finally growing up after all, huh?"
Emiliano gestured towards the woods behind
Dane's mansion. "Let's walk."
I hesitated.

Gunshots erupted—

Startled, I gazed around frantically.

Chill, pussy! It's just a rowdy hip-hop track.

Emiliano put his arm around me. "Just pretend you love me."

Emiliano and his soldiers led me deep into the woods. My legs felt heavy as if they were in iron chains.

What a fucking dummy!

When I had the chance, I should've hijacked a plane to Timbuktu.

Emiliano stood behind me, both judge and executioner.

A terrifying silence–

Emiliano reached into his jacket–

I freaked the fuck out, bolting into the woods.

I prayed the darkness of night would be my ally–

But no!

I was trapped!

Stuck in a dead end. A ravine surrounded by enormous boulders.

As I searched frantically for an escape, Emiliano tackled me to the ground.

His crew kicked and punched me till I was numb.

I tried desperately to protect my face but Eyez kicked me square in the head, knocking the bandage off my nose.

I screamed in pain. Gooey-pus-infested blood dripped down my nostrils.

"What you holding, little bunny?"

I pulled out an envelope. Emiliano ripped into it, counting the bills. "Only another seventeen hundred?"

"If only you'd be more like me, Cody. A big opening came up in Isla Vista. I wish I could've given it to you. But you disappointed me."

My legs went numb as I realized his plan was never to kill me but instead – just the opposite – to give me a fucking promotion!

"Just please! Lemme leave town! I promise I'll get on a bus and never return."

"I really thought I could help you. But clearly, I wasn't up to the challenge."

Emiliano pulled out his 9MM automatic and aimed at my head.

"You should've gone to college after all."

Suddenly, the screams and hooting got louder as a platoon of cheerleaders emerged, surrounding Emiliano and his gang. Emiliano's henchmen quickly hid their weapons, watching in disbelief as Tinker Bell grabbed my hand, "CODY! There you are, baby doll! You promised you were gonna do that awesome trick for everyone."

I never was so glad to see Tinker Bell's movie star face and porn star body.

"We're just borrowing him a few minutes," Tinker Bell tried her best to charm Emiliano. "Then you can have him back. Promise."

The girls encircled me.

There was nothing Emiliano and his soldiers could do as the cheerleaders led me back to the swimming pool.

CHAPTER FORTY-FOUR

Houdini Hot Tub

12:12 am

ane watched nervously as I stepped onto the diving board holding a microphone. "Enjoying my party? Getting fucked up?"

The crowd burped out a few cheers.

A drunk punk yelled, "Show us your vagina or shut the hell up!"

"Alright, you animals. I promised these lovelies I'd give 'em a little entertainment! C'mon, look how fucking hot these incredible babes are!" I motioned to Tinker Bell.

She began kissing her fellow cheerleader, Briana. The party crowd roared their approval.

Finally, Tinker Bell disengaged her lips from the luscious Briana, blowing another big, wet, juicy one to the crowd.

"We want you, Cody!" some chick yelled.

"Show us your dick!" another screamed.

"I got something better than a dick."

"Two dicks? He has two dicks!"

"My dear Tinker Bell, will you please?" I walked to the edge of the diving board. Tinker Bell followed. The board bobbed up and down like a seesaw. She carefully tied me up with rusty, metal chains. Then she wrapped the chains around heavy sandbags.

"My dear friends!" I yelled, "I'm about to attempt something that's never been done in Dane's semen-filled pool. I'm gonna jump in with these super-heavy chains and sandbags dragging me to the bottom. Where I'll either escape... or I'll run out of oxygen."

Emiliano whispered to his crew. I watched them spread around the pool, blocking any escape.

What the fuck was I doing? Just reciting some nonsense I heard at the circus? For real, how many more terrible ideas can I crank out today? As I hesitated, the crowd heckled: "Do it, pussy!" "C'mon, loser!" "Squid ain't gonna fucking do it!"

Eyez nudged Emiliano. "No way he gets outta this alive."

"It's all cause and effect."

"Another law of physics?"

"The jungle," Emiliano said. "Fuck up... YOU DIE."

I lingered for a long moment at the edge of the diving board. I can't... I shouldn't... You know that stupid phrase, 'go big or go home?' Well, I got no fucking home to go to.

The thought of home conjured up an image of my mother. I pictured her, along with her bad-ass Eskimo relatives crossing the Bering Strait.

The first humans EVER—

To walk the unwalkable.

And fuck, that must've been brutal. Every step they must've dreamed of quitting. But then they never would've been the first humans to step foot onto the Americas!

I looked down at the pool and suddenly, everything seemed doable.

I let out a ferocious war cry.

Jumped into the water.

Instantly, I knew something was horribly wrong when my head smashed against the cement.

My body jerked violently as blood spurted out from my skull. An army of red bubbles raced to the surface.

The crowd gasped.

I fought desperately, yanking on the chains.

Nothing!

Void of oxygen, I swallowed a huge gulp of water down my lungs.

Tinker Bell screamed, "SOMEONE HELP HIM!!"

Everyone looked frantic except Emiliano. The bastard cracked a tiny smile.

"MORON!" Dane jumped in. He struggled to untie me from the chains. The rusted metal was stuck. Finally, it snapped open—

Dane heaved my body toward the surface, tossing me onto the deck.

My face turned blue.

The crowd was devastated.

"Is he still breathing?"

CHAPTER FORTY-FIVE

Heaven On Earth

12:18 am

ane stopped pounding on my chest to check for a pulse. "He's fading fast!" Dane frantically administered CPR, breathed into my mouth.

"CALL 9-1-1!" Dane shouted, "NOW!"

"Can you believe your luck?" Emiliano turned to Eyez. "Fucking idiot did our dirty work for us."

CHAPTER FORTY-SIX

Milk the Clock

12:21 am

irls cried. The rest of the crowd had a vacant, far-away look in their eyes. An ambulance and fire truck, lights swirling, screeched onto the scene. Police sirens ripped through the night. Everyone rushed to get the hell out of there as an army of cops swarmed the estate.

"C'mon, you piece of shit!" Dane tried to shake me back to life. "Don't you fucking do this!"

Two paramedics rushed over with a stretcher and defibrillator pack.

One of them looked familiar—

Butt-Crack Benito, the long-haired Argentinian.

He checked me for a pulse. "What you idiots let him do?"

"He gonna make it?" Dane asked

Benito swallowed, "I don't know."

"There's no pulse! He's freezing cold!" voices shouted. "He stopped breathing."

"He could've had it all. Money, riches, success," Emiliano shook his head, more emotional than he wanted his men to see him. "I'm—I'm really—after all the opportunities I gave him. What a fucking fool!"

CHAPTER FORTY-SEVEN

Kick the Devil

12:22 am

he ambulance ripped down the impossibly steep hills of Cito.

"Ventricular fibrillation!" Benito's spirits sunk as he inspected the heart monitor. A chaotic wave of spikes and dips flashed across the screen. "He's fucking dead!!"

"Do something!" Dane shouted.

"I told you it was too fucking dangerous. Why the hell didn't you listen to me?"

"We did! He took the pill just like you said to turn his skin blue. To look dead. But he smashed his fucking head!"

"Then why didn't you pull him out right away?!" Benito grabbed the defibrillator paddles and shoved them against my chest. "CLEAR!!"

My body convulsed with electricity. Benito, covered in sweat, recharged the paddles and slammed them against My chest.

BOOM.

Another tidal wave of electricity.

Benito eyed the monitor.

One beat—

Then another—

The rhythm sped up. Benito jacked an I.V. into my arm and shot me up with Lidocaine. "Level out! C'mon, c'mon, play with me!"

Finally, after several long, torturous moments, the blue drained from my skin.

CHAPTER FORTY-EIGHT

Eighteen Forever

12:23 am

 bolted up, coughing violently. A disgusting wad of bloody mucus trickled down my chin. I vomited gooey-orange bile like a hurricane from Satan.

"You're a God now, bro." Dane patted me gently on the back. "Only immortals cheat death."

"You're motherfucking stupid!" Benito screamed. "Half a mil-
lisecond. Maybe... that's all you had."

I smiled faintly. "Plenty of time."

"I'm serious. You keep flirting with the edge, one day that
black hole's gonna suck you in before you can hit eject!"

"Now, I'd pay to see that!" I snapped up, brimming with life
again. Benito was disappointed I wouldn't give him the satisfac-
tion of admitting he was right.

He wanted me to show emotion and tell him I would be forever a changed man. That I wouldn't be such a cock-tease as I
danced with the Devil.

He doesn't understand what I've come to learn so well—
That adrenaline junkies, like me, live for chaos.

CHAPTER FORTY-NINE

Broken
Middle Finger

5:17 am

The first light of the day slowly ebbed into the world.
Another impenetrable blanket of fog strangled the
city into submission.
I blasted through downtown up to La Mesa residential
community.
I spotted Sajda's beat-up Volvo in the driveway.
I gazed up at her window.

My heart skipped a beat as her light switch flipped on.

Thank God! She's home!

I called her phone for the twentieth time. Again, she didn't pick up. After ruining her photo shoot, I wasn't stupid enough to think she wanted to chat with me. But, since she was pregnant, I didn't think she'd shut me out completely either. Was she up there? High in her ivory tower?

Does she really want me to beg her to lower her hair?

So I can climb up like Rapunzel?

My desperation turned to rage—

"Saj, let me in! I gotta talk to you!" I pounded on the front door and rang the bell a million times. I punched the wood so hard I thought I'd break the damn thing off the hinges. "I've come to some really mature, big thoughts and I've gotta share 'em with you."

Desperate, I picked up a rock to break a window.

And I was really gonna do it! Suddenly—

Sajda's father, Masjid, grabbed me. "Down, Cody! PUT IT DOWN!" Masjid pinned my arms behind my back.

"Where is Sajda? You're hiding her? So not cool! I gotta see her."

"I'm so glad she's finished with you," Masjid said. "I got goose-bumps when she told me that you didn't get into a single school near her."

Even though I wanted to kill him, his candor surprised me.

"Did she tell you who's paying for her college?"

I shook my head no.

"I set up a secret account when she was born." Masjid showed me his Wells Fargo Banking App. "One hundred and forty thousand should get her through her second year of grad school."

I was flabbergasted. "When did you pull a one hundred and eighty with the idea of her studying fashion?"

"Cody, you really think my eyes are sewn shut? I've known for years about her secret fashion sketchbooks.

"And as hard as it is for me to say this because the very idea of you with my daughter makes me cringe. But, I'll admit, without you encouraging, pushing and motivating her, she never would have had the courage to pursue her dream and go to New York."

Masjid put a gentle hand on my shoulder. "I wasn't much different from you once."

"You mean, you weren't always such a cold-hearted cyborg?"

"Back in Pakistan, I must've broken every law in the Koran. I wouldn't drink water—only rum. I chewed Khat, a horrible, speed-like plant that destroys your teeth and rots your brain. And for fun—what we used to call 'partying'—we'd fight the police. With spears, homemade rifles and pipe-bombs. You want to hear the worst part? All of my 'bad friends,' guess what happened to them?"

"Dead?"

"Or in jail. That's why it was a miracle I escaped prison. I thought for sure they'd catch and torture me."

Masjid took off his keffiyeh head scarf, showing me a ring of scars around his scalp. "In my escape from Hell, I promised to keep Sajda far away from people like you."

I wanted to tell Masjid that I wasn't a bad guy. That actually I was a drug-dealing hero—protecting my friends from tainted drugs. But, somehow, it all felt like complete bullshit.

"If you ever really want my blessing, you must drastically alter every aspect of your life."

I wanted to respond with my usually smart-aleck schlock, but my trigger finger was frozen. *Here was a real man, finally talking to me like I didn't still wet my pants.*

Masjid—I always thought him such a conservative prick—but now he'd flipped my lid like he was flipping flapjacks on a grill. What would life have been like if he'd raised me? Better to have a tough bastard, right? Than an alcoholic madman who sneaks whiskey in a baby bottle?

CHAPTER FIFTY

Never Grow Up

wandered the beach. A lost nomad. The waves crashed endlessly. The eternal clock. I dipped my head into the salty ocean, washing my dirty wound. My broken nose stung like a ferocious scorpion bite. I gritted my teeth, absorbing the pain.

After watching a pair of dolphins skip along the waves, I spotted a blurry figure jogging through the mist.

SAJDA.

I hurried out of the surf to catch up to her. "You're like a German train. Right on time."

Sajda turned, surprised to see me. "What would you know? You've never been out of the USA."

"So? I read a lot."

"The Anarchist Cookbook? Skateboard blogs?"

I smiled slightly. "I read every comic in a New Yorker once."

"You still high? Don't you ever get bored of being a complete wastoid?"

"Listen, I thought mad long about our little situation and I know what we need to—"

"Is this really your stupid-ass way of saying sorry for wrecking my shoot?"

Even now I had to look away. I couldn't apologize.

"I'm trying to set up an awesome future for myself, Cody. And, let's face it, you just wanna do as many drugs as you can."

"I know, I've screwed up many times. I haven't always been your best friend." I pulled out a thick envelope from my backpack. "I guess this is my way of apologizing, too. For everything. Please, take it."

She examined the envelope crammed full of wrinkled twenties, tens, fives, and lots of folded, faded George Washingtons.

"This will pay for the procedure. All the doctors. Everything."

"You and I, not only are we out of sync, we aren't even in the same universe anymore."

I should've just let Emiliano kill me. "That's ridiculous, Saj. We, uh, belong together! We're the same person!"

She handed the money back, but I wouldn't take it. The envelope dropped onto the sand.

I watched her turn and walk away.

The walk turned into a jog. Then a sprint. As if she wanted to get away from me as fast as possible.

My eyes moistened as I felt something burning on my back. The sun. Rising. Here it was.

A new day.

Maybe Sajda's right?

I gotta grow the fuck up, get out of Santa Barbara and start a real life.

But first–

I gotta stop getting so damn high all the time.

CHAPTER FIFTY-ONE

Born to Run

I pounded the Xerox machine over and over again. "Why won't you just work dammit??" I pressed every button in every possible combo. Reloaded all the paper trays. An administrative assistant dropped another massive stack of papers. "It's still not fixed? These gotta be copied by tomorrow."

I gazed at the huge piles of copying and binders to be bound and proof-checked by the morning. A staggering amount of work. Although, It was almost 5PM on a Friday and almost everyone had left the office already, I knew I was gonna be here way past dinner.

That means I'm long overdue for a smoke break, right?

I mashed outside, zipping up my jacket. It was my first real winter. A massive Alaskan storm ripped along the Cascades, focusing its fury on the Northwest.

I was almost finished with my semester working for the Dean in the admissions office at Oregon State. When I showed up out of the blue, begging him to reinstate my scholarship, he laughed before offering me a tough deal—intern for his secretary for a whole semester. I had to prove I was serious about coming back to school.

Of course, I had to come here under a pseudonym so Emiliano couldn't find me. But the Dean, when I told him about the situation, was a decent guy and more than willing to help.

To make a few extra bucks, I did a huge mural for a local music studio. They only gave me $75 which barely covered the spray cans.

It got me high. And not just from the paint fumes.

I was doing street art legally.

I loved it.

weeks later:

A long-haired hipster with a golf cap bounced down the administration steps and asked to borrow my lighter. I was surprised to see the disheveled young man light up a joint right in front of the Dean's office! He offered me a hit. I checked the calendar on my smart watch. "Exactly one hundred and eighty-six days since I've taken a rip, snort, or swallow of anything."

"Must be nice not losing your wallet every damn day." The dude whipped out a flyer for an upcoming fiesta. "My best friend's band's playing! They rip! Come meet some of the local musicians—you'll dig all the weirdoes."

CHAPTER FIFTY-TWO

Mr. Somebody

The fiesta was cool except it felt like one giant test. A mirror up to my face. And although there wasn't a fat line of my favorite Kitty Kat waiting—it was a delicious smelling joint. Or perfect cocaine lines. *Or the blond in the corner dipping molly onto her tongue.*

A madman arrived wearing a poncho. Guy was dropping sugar cubes of liquid LSD in everyone's mouth like we were back in the free-loving sixties chasing Ken Kesey's magic school bus full of Merry Pranksters. Everyone hooted, hollered and cheered for this hero. .

Everyone opened their mouths, hoping for the DEALER WITH NO NAME to pop in a freebie. Every girl wanted to hug him. Every dude wanted to shake his hand.

Fuck yes, I was jealous!

I remembered how amazing it felt—blasting into a party and setting everyone's heart on fire! Those are the moments I lived for! Shit, usually the party didn't start until I waltzed in with a super-size bag of party favors.

Suddenly, I felt overwhelmingly alone. I trudged outside into the fresh air, letting the snow sprinkle across my tongue.

Incoming video message. I was pleasantly surprised to see a video of Dane back with his Army unit. He beat the court martial. "Just like you needed a Guardian Angel, these Iraqis need a babysitter, too!" In the video, he was teaching Iraqi soldiers how to use a grenade launcher.

BOOM.

I shuddered thinking about what he told me the last time we spoke.

"Emiliano knows you're still alive, Cody."

"Who gives a fuck about tomorrow, right? Besides, nobody knows where I am except you."

"Emiliano would have to take a plane halfway around the world. And even if he waterboarded my ass—I would never, ever give you up."

I knew it was true. Dane would gladly take a bullet for me.

He's said so a million times and that's why I love the bastard.

Speaking of love—I missed Santa Barbara.

I pulled out my antique compass.

Even though I never once got it to work properly, I just liked holding it because it reminded me of my sister.

But most of all—

I missed Sajda.

I desperately wanted to hear her voice.

Even if just for a second.

But she still wanted me dead. Maybe even more so than Emi-liano.

Sometimes, when you burn that bridge, there's no rebuild-ing—even with a slave army and a few dragons.

I'm assuming she had the abortion—but I don't even know. Could she have possibly kept our kid?

I couldn't help myself.

I called her.

Voicemail.

"Yo, Saj, I just wanted to tell you that I really miss the crap out of you. I know that once a little time goes by... maybe, just maybe... you can, uh...." Suddenly, I felt very fragile. "I hope you're good. Send me a picture or email... anything."

I was about to hang up when I paused, staring at the phone. Fuck, that's lame.

I punched erase and deleted that sappy message from exist-ence. Loud sirens took over the night. Everyone at the party ran out. I was still on probation in California and wasn't technically allowed to be in Oregon. After all the progress I'd made in the last few months, I didn't wanna see no Joe Cop set me back.

So I hid the best I could, crouching in a shower. I saw the drug dealer hide his drugs in the sink cabinet. As cops moved through the house, he must have panicked and bolted.

Finally, convinced the cops were gone, I bravely eased out of the shower and washed my face in the sink.

A sharp elbow hit me in the back. I assumed it was the drug dealer back to retrieve his stash. But no, instead, I was pleasant-ly surprised to meet two lovely coeds. Both scantily-clad, both with that dangerous glint in their eyes. Like one too many blinks and who knows, Dorothy, we might just end up in a Vegas Suite.

The blond asked in the sexiest voice I ever heard. "We're freshman and don't have many friends. Wanna party with us?"

I stared at the drugs behind the toilet paper.

What?

Am I supposed to tell you I did the right thing? That I left the stash of drugs and ditched the mesmerizing babes for a poetry reading of Ginsberg's Howl?

Is that really gonna get my adrenaline pumping???

I pulled out the bag of drugs and examined all the different chemicals and powders gleaming in the dim, yellowish light. The blond whispered seductively in my ear, "I wanna see the fucking Devil. Can you take me there?"

www.ingramcontent.com/pod-product-compliance
Lightning Source LLC
Chambersburg PA
CBHW070844120626
46556CB00002B/873